'I want som

Cristiano's dark ~~~~~~~~~~~~~~ vet trailing over silk.

Her heart jumped behind her breastbone. She met bold dark golden eyes shaded by luxuriant black lashes. Breathing normally became a distinct challenge. His lean dark features were wholly intent on her. Something that felt like a tiny hot wire was pulling taut in her pelvis. It was a sensation that fell somewhere between pleasure and pain, and the surge of heat that followed made her tremble.

His sizzling sexy smile slashed his beautiful mouth. 'And I do believe you will enjoy giving it to me, *cara mia.*'

Lydia was finding it impossible to concentrate. 'I'm afraid I don't understand—'

'Don't you? I'm offering a pretty basic deal. I want you in my bed.'

For Love or MONEY

This is romance on the red carpet…

For Love or Money is the ultimate reading experience for the reader who loves Modern, and who also has a taste for tales of wealth and celebrity and the accompanying gossip and scandal!

Look out for the special covers in Modern Romance™

MISTRESS BOUGHT AND PAID FOR

BY
LYNNE GRAHAM

MILLS & BOON®

First published in Great Britain 2006
Harlequin Mills & Boon Limited,
Eton House, 18-24 Paradise Road, Richmond, Surrey TW9 1SR

© Lynne Graham 2006

ISBN-13: 978 0 263 84840 3
ISBN-10:   0 263 84840 X

Set in Times Roman 10½ on 12¾ pt.
01-0906-49866

Printed and bound in Spain
by Litografia Rosés, S.A., Barcelona

MISTRESS
BOUGHT AND
PAID FOR

CHAPTER ONE

CRISTIANO ANDREOTTI, the software billionaire, stood on the topmost deck of the megayacht *Lestara*. Built to his exacting specifications, and already regarded as the most beautiful craft ever built, *Lestara* was a floating palace, complete with twin helipads, a cinema, a freshwater swimming pool and a sleek landing craft tucked in her stern. Yet Cristiano was infuriatingly conscious of the faintest tinge of disappointment with his latest acquisition.

His guests, however, were talking about the yacht in hushed tones of reverence.

'Unbelievable…'

'The most staggering level of luxury I've ever seen…'

'You have a private hospital and you're *never* ill…*wow*, is all I can say…'

'The gym and the basketball court are to die for…'

'The glass viewing area in the hull blew me away…'

'Sixty crew members to sail her and wait on you…you must feel like a king…'

His lean, darkly handsome profile detached, his brilliant dark eyes bleak, Cristiano continued to look out to sea. A king? Not so as he had noticed. He wondered if he had brought company on board to say for him what he no longer said or felt himself. Increasingly, only aggressive takeovers or extreme sports gave Cristiano a genuine buzz. Born into fabulous wealth, he had discovered that few experiences, or indeed possessions, lived up to their initial promise.

'Have you heard the gossip?' the socialite Jodie Morgan was asking in her piercing English upper-class voice when he emerged from his reverie. 'About Lia Powell?' she continued.

As Cristiano tensed at the unexpected sound of that name, female giggles broke out.

'There are rumours all around London. How do you think she'll take to life in prison?'

'Who are you talking about?' his friend, Philip Hazlett, enquired.

'The Powell girl…that model who took off with Mort Stevens. Her career dive-bombed when he was done for drugs and she disappeared off the map,' Jodie reminded her fiancé cheerfully. 'A couple of months ago she tried to make a comeback by doing good works—'

'Yes. I believe she organised a fashion show for some children's charity called Happy Holidays and made a mess of it,' Philip interposed in a suggestive tone of finality.

Impervious to the hint that the subject matter might not be welcome, Jodie continued to tell the story. 'Lia persuaded her fellow models to donate their services free to the show, and the goss is she robbed the poor little kiddies blind by pocketing the proceeds!'

A spark of raw splintering gold flared in Cristiano's brooding, dark gaze. He was grimly amused by Philip's attempt to silence Jodie. Evidently the socialite was not aware that Lia Powell and Cristiano had briefly been an item. For a nanosecond time leapt back eighteen months, to Cristiano's first glimpse of Lia Powell during a Paris show. Slender and sinuous as a willow wand, she had stalked down the catwalk like a warrior princess, her pale blonde hair rippling back from her hauntingly lovely face like silvery streamers of moonlight. Huge eyes the mesmeric blue of lapis lazuli had blanked him when he was introduced. Her smile had been a masterpiece of indifference. Accustomed to instant awe and fawning attention, Cristiano had been intrigued, his lust heightened by that rare sense of being challenged. He had been eager to see just how well she played a game he had assumed was naïvely aimed at increasing his interest.

But, unusually, Cristiano had underestimated the brazen avarice and ambition of his scheming target. Although he had been unaware of it, he had not been the only wealthy male in Lia's sights, and she had been chasing a better offer than a casual affair. After a handful of dates he had invited her to his country house for the weekend. There Lia had come over all virginal and refused to share his suite. At dawn the following day, however, she had eloped with one of his guests: a dissolute rock star more than twice her age, famous for his very expensive habit of marrying his youthful arm-candy. As he chirpily introduced Lia to the press as his new fiancée, Mort Stevens must have seemed the more rewarding prospect in financial terms. Unhappily for Lia, though, cruel fate had intervened to ensure that all her plotting and planning had come to nothing in the end.

With an almost imperceptible signal, Cristiano inclined his imperious dark head and his watchful PA hurried over to receive his instructions. While his guests were served with lunch on the entertainment deck Cristiano was in his office, being briefed with the facts he needed. A discreet phone call to a national newspaper editor revealed, in the time-honoured phrase beloved of the tabloids, that Lia was 'helping the police with their enquiries'. But soon everyone would know the *real* story. Who could have sympathy for a woman accused of defrauding underprivileged children?

A slow, hard-edged smile of satisfaction slashed Cristiano's bold, masculine mouth. He was conscious of an energy surge of pure badness. All boredom had fled. It was said that revenge was a dish best eaten cold, but Cristiano was more into hot and spicy flavours. While she'd played for time eighteen months ago, Lia Powell had faked prudish innocence to stay out of his bed. She had then, with breathtaking impudence, cheated on him beneath his own roof. She was the only woman who had *ever* said no to Cristiano and walked out on him. He knew that the secret of her lingering attraction in his mind could only be that basic.

When it came to sex, Cristiano knew himself inside out. He was much more clued up than his late father, whose life had been destroyed by his hopeless addiction to a woman with as much heart as a carcass on a butcher's block. He had even fewer illusions about Lia Powell. She was a worthless little scrubber with no morals. But she was still a bloody gorgeous one, he mused with ruthless cool, and for the price of her freedom she could be his. He had no doubt of that fact. Any charity would prefer recompense and a handsome donation over an indiscreet and costly court case. He could buy Lia Powell's pardon. He could buy *her*. He had never paid for sex before. Did he want her on such tacky terms? He discovered that the very thought of having leggy Lia tangled within his sheets and eager to please excited him more than anything had in a very long time. She would be on call whenever he so desired, to provide easy and uncomplicated sexual release.

He was willing to acknowledge that where women were concerned he had a low boredom threshold. In fact he was notorious for the brevity of his relationships. But this would be something different—something new and fresh. A contractual agreement would be the best blueprint for such an arrangement. His lawyers would relish that novel challenge almost as much as he would revel in having Lia act out his every tacky fantasy…

The young bespectacled solicitor gave Lydia a troubled look. 'I can't help you if you won't help yourself.'

Lydia dropped her head, weariness engulfing her. 'I know…'

'You must protect yourself,' he warned her equally wearily.

'Not if that means my mother taking the blame,' Lydia countered in a tight, driven voice. 'This is nothing to do with her and I won't have her involved.'

'But as co-signatory on the cheques she *is* involved,' the solicitor pointed out flatly. 'Naturally the police want to speak to her as well.'

Lydia said nothing. During the preceding long and nerve-racking interview with two officers she had been asked repeatedly where her mother, Virginia Carlton, was. Nobody had believed her when she'd said she didn't know, and she had tried not to care. After all, even if she had known she would have protected the older woman by keeping her whereabouts a secret. She was determined not to let her mother pay the price for her daughter's mistakes.

Now, one of the fraud officers reappeared. He told her that, although she was to be released on bail while more enquiries were made, she would have to return to the station in four days' time for further questioning. Even as her heart sank at that assurance, Lydia was informed that she would have to leave the interview room and wait in a cell for the necessary paperwork to be prepared. Her tummy flipped in dismay. Her solicitor protested, but to no avail.

The cell door was mercifully closed on her before a violent fit of shaking overtook her tall, slender frame. Sinking down on the hard sleeping platform, Lydia wrapped trembling arms round herself in an effort to get a grip. There was no point in giving way to the fear and the panic pulling at her. Matters were only going to get worse, she reminded herself heavily. The wheels of justice were grinding into motion to prosecute and punish her, and if she was found guilty she would serve a prison sentence. Eventually the sight of a cell would be very familiar to her. The money from the Happy Holidays account was gone, and she could neither repay it nor borrow it. The conviction that she could only blame herself for that state of affairs hit her hard.

Her thin shoulders slumped, guilt racking her. It was a familiar feeling. Things always went horribly wrong, and it seemed that it was her fault…

When Lydia had been ten years old she had survived a boating accident in which her father and her kid brother had drowned. Her mother, Virginia, had been distraught. 'This is your fault!' she had screamed furiously at her daughter. 'Who was it who begged and begged to go on that stupid boat trip? You killed them. You killed the two of them!'

And, even though other people had hushed the hysterical older woman, Lydia had known that her grieving parent was only speaking the unpalatable truth. Then, when her father's business had gone bankrupt, and their comfortable standard of living had vanished overnight, Lydia had known that she was to blame for that as well. It had been a huge relief when she'd discovered just a few years later that she had the earning power to give that luxury lifestyle back to her mother. Between the ages of fourteen and twenty-one Lydia had made a small fortune as a model.

But then, Lydia acknowledged wretchedly, she had become selfish—stupidly, wickedly selfish. And short-sighted. She'd hated modelling, and a bad experience and a broken heart had persuaded her to leave the fashion world behind and train as a garden designer. Everything that since had gone wrong could be traced back to that single foolish and fanciful decision…

Still in fear of the press cameras that had greeted her arrival at the police station, Lydia walked stiffly out to the reception area. Thankfully the only person to show the slightest interest in her appearance was the small curvaceous brunette seated there. Her cousin Gwenna stood up, frowning when she saw the exhaustion etched on Lydia's face. Yet the younger woman still looked so incredibly beautiful that even Gwenna found it hard not to stare. The pure lines of Lydia's delicate bone structure, allied to her dazzling blue eyes and the mane of naturally pale blonde hair, took most people's breath away.

'Gwenna?' Lydia was dismayed that the other woman had subjected herself to the embarrassment of coming to the police station on her behalf. 'You shouldn't have come—'

'Don't be silly,' Gwenna scolded her in Welsh as she marched her much taller cousin out into the night and on to the car park, with her head held high and her chin at a determined angle, defying the camera flashes. 'You're family—and where else should I be? I'm here to take you home—'

Lydia was too touched by Gwenna's appearance to be able to find the right words in Welsh, a language that she had only recently rediscovered. She swallowed hard on the thickness in her throat and climbed into Gwenna's ancient hatchback. As a young child she had often stayed in Gwenna's Welsh-speaking home while her own parents were abroad. Eighteen months back, when Lydia's life had been in awful turmoil, Gwenna had phoned to invite her to use the family farm as a bolthole. The generous warmth of that offer had meant a great deal to Lydia at a time when her friends had abandoned her.

'I really appreciate you doing this, but I think you should forget that you know me for a while—'

'I'll just pretend I didn't hear that,' Gwenna interposed, in probably much the same no-nonsense tone that she employed with the teenagers she taught. In her early thirties, she had short dark hair that shone as though it had been polished.

When Lydia unlocked the door of the tiny terraced house where she now lived, Gwenna headed straight for the kitchen. 'I'll make a cup of tea while you nip upstairs and pack a bag.'

Lydia stiffened. 'No, I'm not coming home with you. This is a small community and you have to live and work here. You mustn't get caught up in my problems.'

Gwenna turned. 'Lydia—'

'No…' Fierce conviction made Lydia's soft voice unusually firm. 'I mean it. Think of your father. He's barely over the loss of your mother. Let's not upset him with this as well.'

The brunette's look of disconcertion told Lydia that she had stumbled on the one argument that would work—for Gwenna was protective of her elderly parent.

'But thanks for caring,' Lydia tacked on gently.

Sudden anger brightened Gwenna's troubled gaze. 'But it's not a matter of caring. You didn't take that money and we all know who did!'

Her colour fluctuating at that assertion, Lydia breathed, 'Maybe you *think* you know—'

'Come off it! You're so straight you can't tell a lie without crossing your fingers!' her cousin told her impatiently. 'Do you expect me to keep quiet while you take the rap for a woman who couldn't care less about you?'

Losing colour at that blunt statement, Lydia switched on the kettle. Gwenna had never been able to understand the nature of Lydia's relationship with her mother. The brunette's family had been blessed with a quiet and secure lifestyle, while Virginia had survived tragedy and a succession of thoroughly unreliable men that would have broken a lesser woman. 'My mother has had a very tough life—'

'Look, she was telling you that when you were five years old, making you fetch and carry like a little slave while she moaned about the horrors of motherhood. And let's not overlook the fact that between them your mother and your stepfather have managed to spend every penny you ever earned!'

There was reproach in Lydia's troubled gaze. 'You can't blame them because the nightclub failed and I lost everything last year. I was naïve about the amount of money I'd made as a model. I thought it would last a lifetime—'

'It would have done if you had only been keeping yourself, and not Virginia and Dennis with their huge house and flash cars. I can't believe that you had the slightest personal interest in opening a nightclub either.' Her companion sighed.

Lydia said nothing. When she had stopped modelling she had effectively dispossessed her stepfather of his job managing her career and her money. Agreeing to provide the capital for a nightclub had seemed the least she could do. Sadly, the enterprise had crashed. But Lydia had come to terms with the loss of her financial security. Although she was only twenty-two years old, she was well used to picking herself up after a disappointment.

Busily engaged in making tea, Gwenna was wishing that she could get her hands on Lydia's greedy mother and thieving stepfather. Given the chance she would soon tell them what she thought of them! The couple had turned Lydia into the family cash cow, and had enjoyed the high life on the lucrative proceeds of her modelling career. Although Virginia had never worked herself, she had always been able to spend like there was no tomorrow.

'You have to deal with this,' Gwenna told her cousin impatiently. 'Virginia stole the money you raised from the fashion show and spent it—'

Lydia shook her head in tired disagreement. 'Dennis had left her with a pile of debts. She knew I couldn't help and she panicked.'

'Stop making excuses for her. She forged your signature on the cheques that emptied the Happy Holidays account. She did everything she could to make you look like the guilty party, and now she's done a runner! Don't let her do this to you,' Gwenna pleaded in frustration. 'A criminal conviction will wreck your life. How many people will employ an ex-con?'

When Gwenna had gone home, Lydia retrieved the letter that she'd seen lying on her doormat and read it with a growing hollow feeling inside. It was a brief note from a couple who had accepted her quote to design their garden. They would have been her first proper clients since she had completed her college course. But they had dropped this letter through her letterbox earlier today to say that they had changed their minds. She suspected that what had changed their minds had been news of her visit to the local police station. No doubt her face would be all over the tabloids tomorrow morning.

Later, in bed, she tossed and turned. The evening before she'd had to go out to buy food. An odd little pool of silence had seemed to enclose her as she'd packed her groceries at the supermarket. When she'd looked up, a couple of women had been treating her to a contemptuous appraisal. Evidently rumours of the stolen money had already spread to the highly efficient local grapevine. It had been a disturbing experience.

On the edge of an uneasy doze, Lydia was yanked rudely back to full wakefulness by the sound of a crash and glass breaking. Switching on the bedside light, she got out of bed. Had someone smashed a bottle outside on the street? She went downstairs and found the window in her small cosy sitting room broken. She hovered in the doorway, wondering how such a thing could have happened, and then she saw something lying on the floor in the middle of the shattered glass. It was a stone with a piece of paper wrapped round it. Frowning she spread it out to read.

YOU THIEVING BITCH GO BACK TO WHERE
YOU BELONG!

The brutal capitals were written in red felt-tip. Her heart started to hammer like crazy and she felt physically sick. She made herself fetch a brush and dustpan to clean up the glass. She propped an old cupboard door from the coal shed over the gaping hole and slowly climbed back up the stairs. But if sleep had been elusive before, it was now impossible, and she lay still and quiet and barely breathing, flinching at every sound she heard.

Having finally fallen asleep around seven the next morning, she was still in bed when the doorbell went at ten. She assumed that it was the postman and, knowing that he would not wait long, rose in haste, pulling on her cotton wrap and racing downstairs to answer the door.

As her stunned gaze took in the very tall black-haired male outside on the street, she was gripped by total disbelief and pinned to the spot in complete stillness. Cristiano Andreotti. Even though she thought he could only be a figment of her imagination, the compelling effect of his exotic dark charisma and hard-edged masculinity still knocked her for six. Her heart started pounding and her soft pink mouth opened on a soundless *ooh*.

His magnificent bone structure was accentuated by the smooth olive planes of his high cheekbones. Although he shaved twice daily, faint blue-black shading still emphasised his strong jaw and beautifully modelled mouth. But her mind refused to move on from recognition to acceptance. Because Cristiano Andreotti did not belong on the doorstep of a terraced house in the back street of a nondescript Welsh market town. His natural milieu was much more exclusive, and always redolent of the privilege of the very rich.

Cristiano studied her with unflinching intensity. He had never seen her without make-up before. He saw the changes in her, picked up on every flaw with the eagerness of a man who had dimly expected and possibly even hoped to be disappointed in her. She had lost weight. She was pale, and her tiredness was patent. Her mane of fair hair fell in a tangle round her slight shoulders, no longer glossy and styled into smooth layers of silk by a professional hand. In the midst of cataloguing those differences with the precision of a male to whom no detail was too small, he met eyes as blue as sapphires. Just as suddenly he realised that she was, if anything, more breathtakingly beautiful than ever. Only this time around she was as nature had made her, with glorious eyes, skin like clotted cream and full, pouting mouth. Desire ripped through his big powerful frame with the dangerous force of a storm tide.

'May I come in?' he enquired lazily, his rich, resonant drawl wrapping round her rigid spinal cord like a silk caress. The habit of command and high expectation was so engrained in every syllable that it did not even occur to her to deny him.

CHAPTER TWO

ONLY when Cristiano broke the pounding silence could Lydia credit the reality of his appearance. Snatching in a startled breath, she blinked, her long brown lashes fluttering as she struggled to get a hold on the bone-deep shock gripping her. Even in that very first moment she knew that the flame of her hatred for him burned as bright as ever. Perspiration beaded her short upper lip and her legs felt wobbly. She stared fixedly at him, controlled by a heady mixture of fear and fascination, curiosity and loathing.

Predictably, Cristiano took advantage of her astonishment to move forward, and she automatically retreated. Although she was five foot eleven in her bare feet, he still towered over her by a comfortable six inches. A snaking little frisson of awareness curled somewhere low in her belly, and she went rigid at the novelty of that almost forgotten sensation. All senses on hyper-alert, she could feel the tender tips of her breasts tingle and pinch.

Hot colour flared through her pallor as shame and confusion filled her, and suddenly she found her voice. 'What do you want?'

Cristiano closed the front door with a casual, lean

brown hand. He was feeling his power and enjoying it. 'Don't you know?'

Painfully embarrassed by the way her treacherous body had reacted to him, Lydia tilted her chin in a defiant manner that would have surprised any one of her relatives. She felt trapped and angry and raw. Deep down inside her lurked the wounding recollection of just how much she had once cared for Cristiano Andreotti and how savagely he had hurt her. It didn't show on the surface, but he had changed her—and not for the better. 'How could I know why you're here?'

'I thought some sixth sense survival instinct might kick in…' Cristiano surveyed her with liquid dark eyes full of mockery. 'Might spell out a simple message.'

'Obviously not.' She folded her arms in a defensive gesture and tried to still the trembling aftershock that was threatening to take her over.

'I'm here because I want to see you…*obviously*,' Cristiano traded, his sexy accent wrapping round the syllables in the most extraordinarily melodic way.

Without having realised what she was doing, Lydia found she was staring up at him, at those brilliant, beautiful dark eyes that had haunted her dreams. Eyes that betrayed only the most superficial emotion and her own reflection. He gave nothing away. He was famous for a detachment that veered on indifference, even icy coldness. She had felt ten feet tall when she'd made him laugh or smile.

Fighting that tide of memory, she shook her head as though to clear it. She strove feverishly to blank him out, remembering fearfully how it had been for her for a crazy couple of months when he had been all she could think about, when his mere presence had been enough to ensure that she was blind to everybody and everything but him.

'I don't want you here…' Even as she spoke, she knew that the remedy of asking him to leave was in her hands, but that for reasons she was afraid to examine she could not yet bring herself to actually tell him to go.

Cristiano angled his sleek dark head to one side and studied her with maddening cool. 'Don't you?'

Her tummy seemed to somersault, as if he had punched a panic button. For a crazy moment she worried that he knew her better than she knew herself, and she rushed to fill the silence. 'How did you find me?'

'I obtained some privileged information…'

She turned pale as milk. So he knew about the missing money. *Of course he knew*, an inner voice censured. She wanted to cringe, and a pronounced reluctance to look him in the face afflicted her.

Cristiano Andreotti took advantage of that moment of weakness and stepped past her. He knew her fortunes had been in a steady decline since their last meeting, but it was only now when he saw the shabby, sparsely furnished sitting room, that he appreciated how steep that descent had been. Nothing could more adequately illustrate the vast gulf between their lives, and the reality that she had only ever been a visitor in his world.

'What happened to the window?'

'It got broken,' she mumbled.

'Have you called a glazier?'

'Not yet. It only happened late last night.'

His incisive gaze alighted on the crudely lettered and crumpled note on the mantelpiece and he reached for it. The stone was sitting on the hearth, and he guessed what had happened. A frown drew his sleek dark brows together for a split second. 'You've been threatened? Have you reported this?'

In an abrupt movement she snatched the abusive note from his shapely brown fingers. 'Why don't you mind your own business?' she gasped, more mortified than ever.

'The police should be told. The brute mentality behind that sort of intimidation is liable to get more physical. You cannot stay here alone—'

'And where do you suggest I move to?' she broke in tautly, deeper anxiety assailing her—for if anything the incident last night had made her even more reluctant to take advantage of her cousin's offer of shelter. Gwenna, and her father and brother, lived in an isolated farmhouse, and she would not risk bringing trouble to their door.

'I may be able to provide a solution,' Cristiano murmured without the slightest change in his level of intonation.

Lydia realised that she was trembling. Looking away from him, she struggled for mastery over conflicting promptings of fear, bewilderment and discomfiture. In doing so, she registered for the first time since his arrival that she was standing in front of him wearing an old dressing gown and with messy hair. She almost died of chagrin.

'Look, I need to get dressed…I'm not going to hang around arguing with you.' *What solution?* she wanted to ask, but she wouldn't let herself. She hadn't even told him to get out. Didn't she have any pride? How much lower could she sink?

Watching her climb the stairs, Cristiano caught a flash of a pale, slender silk-smooth thigh, and an instant shaft of heat travelled to his groin. He ground his even white teeth together. The sexual buzz in the atmosphere was sending his male hormones on a primal rampage. That ferocious attraction had been there from the first time he saw her. But he was convinced that once he slept with her, he would no longer want her. She was scared. If he offered her the money without further ado she would probably let him have her here and now. So what if it was sleazy? So what if he had never paid for the privilege of bedding a woman before? *Dio mio,* she wanted him too. Her eyes and her edginess around him were unmistakably revealing to a male of his experience. Yet she still seemed to be in denial of that truth—always backing off, primly avoiding visual contact. A guy with some class would wait and prolong the finale, he told himself grimly.

A gardening book lay open on the small dining table and he studied it with a questioning frown. Restive as a hungry panther on the prowl, he paced. It was a challenge, for the room was tiny, the hall non-existent and the kitchen not much larger. There, however, he came to a sudden halt, a black brow rising in astonishment. In defiance of the grim urban outlook, the small back yard had been transformed into a glorious green patio jungle of container-ised flowers and foliage.

Employing his mobile phone, he told one of his staff to organise a glazier to replace the broken window. He said the job had to be done immediately.

Upstairs, Lydia darted into the bathroom and ran a brush violently through her tousled hair, while at the same time trying to clumsily clean her teeth. She was all fingers and thumbs as she shed her nightwear and yanked a pair of jeans and a vest top from a drawer. How could she be calm and controlled? Downstairs was the guy who had won her trust and made her love him. Downstairs was the smooth, slick operator who knew how to fake romance and act as if he was serious. But it had all been a con. She had been the victim of his cruel, demeaning charade! A dupe, a joke for macho males who got in touch with their crude masculine selves by comparing the number of notches on their bedposts. She zipped up her jeans with a trembling hand. Unfortunately, she had been so hurt and angered by that betrayal she had made herself a victim all over again. She had fallen for the stupid suggestion that she might take revenge and at least emerge with her pride intact. The consequences of that final foolish impulse had pretty much destroyed her modelling career.

So what was Cristiano Andreotti doing in Wales? Why had he come to see her? A solution? She couldn't see why he would wish to help her in any way. When she'd left his Georgian mansion with Mort she had struck a blow at Cristiano's ego. There had been nothing else to take aim at, she acknowledged painfully. Cristiano Andreotti did not have a heart or a conscience. Had he come to gloat over more of her unending misfortunes?

Slowly, Lydia descended the stairs. 'What do you want with me?' she asked defensively.

'What do most guys want?' Cristiano traded, smooth as glass, while he scanned the silvery pale waves tumbling round her oval face, her luminous blue eyes and her sultry lips, which were slightly parted to show the moist inner pink. He wasn't really listening; he was rejoicing in her visual allure.

Hot colour flooded her cheeks. The direction of his gaze was not lost on her, and she shot him a look of loathing. 'At least you're not pretending to be a nice guy any more!'

Dark eyes flaring to gold, Cristiano inclined his arrogant dark head in acknowledgement. 'You'd take advantage of a nice guy. I'm much more your style.'

'In your dreams!' Lydia slung back at him.

'How often does Mort Stevens figure in yours now?' Cristiano riposted without skipping a beat.

That merciless retort made her blench, and she semi-turned away, presenting him with a view of her delicate profile. 'You still haven't told me what you're doing here.'

Sideways on, her slender build made her look disturbingly fragile. Without hesitation he reached out and closed his hands over hers.

In surprise, she gasped, 'What the heck—?'

'Just checking…' Having scanned her arms for any suspicious marks that might have indicated drug abuse, and satisfied himself that that was not her problem, Cristiano released her again.

'I do *not* do drugs…I never have and I never will!' she protested furiously.

'Glad to hear it.' But she needed to eat more, Cristiano reflected as his attention skimmed from her narrow white shoulders to the pert outline of her small breasts. She wasn't wearing a bra. He tensed, infuriated by his own thoughts and behaviour. What was he? A schoolboy again? Since when had the female form entertained the slightest mystery for him?

'Did you only come here to insult me?'

'No, there is always purpose in what I do. You're facing a prison sentence.'

Taken aback by that unequivocal assurance, Lydia snatched in a sharp breath. 'You don't know that…how could you? You know nothing about it—'

'Crimes that entail cash and deception and female offenders always attract a more severe punishment,' Cristiano murmured silkily. 'Defrauding a charity was not a good idea—particularly one engaged in raising funds for disadvantaged children.'

Her skin felt cold and clammy. 'I don't want to talk about it.'

'Were you in debt? Were you being pursued for payment? You stole a very large amount of money, but I don't see much evidence of ill-gotten gains.'

That Cristiano had no doubt of her culpability cut across Lydia's tender skin like a whiplash. A painful tide of colour lit her face. On the strength of rumour, he had decided that she was guilty as charged.

'Why should you care either way?' she queried, throwing back her pale head, her chin at a truculent angle.

Cristiano surveyed her with eyes as cool and hard as tempered steel. 'I don't. But I *can* keep you out of prison…'

She stiffened, eyes widening, while a crazy little leap of hope surfaced somewhere inside her. 'And how could you possibly do that?'

'By repaying the money you took with the addition of a handsome donation to oil the wheels of charitable forgiveness,' Cristiano explained softly.

'It wouldn't be that simple—'

'Don't be foolish. I never talk about what I can't do.' His wide, sensual mouth curled. 'A discreet approach has already been made to the director of the Happy Holidays fund, and the response to that particular suggestion has been a very positive one.'

Her restive fingers clenched in on themselves with fierce tension. 'But why would you offer to replace the missing cash?'

'Obviously because I want something in return,' Cristiano delivered, soft and low, his dark drawl as erotic as velvet trailing over silk.

Her heart jumped behind her breastbone. She met bold, dark golden eyes shaded by luxuriant black lashes. Breathing normally became a distinct challenge. His lean dark features were wholly intent on her. Something that felt like a tiny hot wire was pulling taut in her pelvis. It was a sensation that fell somewhere between pleasure and pain, and the surge of heat that followed made her tremble.

His sizzling, sexy smile slashed his beautiful mouth. 'And I do believe you will enjoy giving it to me, *cara mia*.'

Lydia was finding it impossible to concentrate. 'I'm afraid I don't understand—'

'Don't you? I'm offering a pretty basic deal. I want you in my bed—'

Shock roared through her, leaving her light-headed. 'I don't believe you—'

'Of course you would have to throw yourself heart and soul into the role of being my mistress—'

'This doesn't make sense—'

His brilliant eyes were ice-cold. 'It makes perfect sense. Watching you endeavour to meet my every wish and need will provide me with considerable entertainment. I'm not an easy guy to please.'

Lydia had turned bone-white. 'You can't despise me and want me like that at the same time.'

'Why not?'

'Because it's immoral!' she gasped.

'When did I say I was moral?'

'I can't believe your nerve. I can't believe you can approach me with such a proposition!' Lydia lanced back at him, burning with furious mortification. 'Maybe you don't have any standards, but I do—'

'I don't steal,' Cristiano proclaimed, in a super-soft undertone.

'Maybe I don't either. But you're only interested in

trying to take advantage of the fact that I'm in trouble, and I think that is disgusting!'

'I've made a fortune from opportunism, *cara mia.*'

'Well, you lucked out when you met me—because I'd sooner go to prison than sink to the level of being your mistress!'

Shimmering dark golden eyes connected with hers. 'I don't think so.'

The force field of energy he projected was all around her, like an invisible web of silent intimidation. Unable to break the hold of his compelling scrutiny, she felt his anger, and it somehow soothed the ache deep down inside her.

'I *know* so.'

As she stepped past him, he curved a light hand to her spine and stilled her. He bent his handsome dark head and the cool, irresistible power of his sensual mouth claimed hers. It was everything she had secretly feared, everything she had ever craved. With the utmost gentleness he let his tongue steal between her parted lips and explore the moist interior. He delved deeper. She moaned low in her throat, heard her own plaintive cry of surrender and acceptance, and wanted to die of shame. But still she couldn't break free of the fierce physical excitement that controlled her. That inner conflict made her quiver, as though she was in the eye of a storm.

Cristiano stepped back. He had not held her. He had not given her that much excuse to succumb. 'Answer the phone…'

Only when she was separated from him did the world crowd back in on her again, and she heard the phone's insistent shrill. She surged in a feverish rush to answer it. Fighting to rescue her smashed composure, but nowhere near strong enough to meet Cristiano's appraisal, Lydia snapped a damp palm round the receiver. It was her solicitor. She stiffened in dismay when she learned that the police had requested a meeting today, rather than in four days' time, as had been previously arranged.

'It's your choice. You don't *have* to go to the station. But evidently they have some new information, and I feel it would be in your best interests to agree to make yourself available today,' her legal adviser informed her.

Lydia breathed in deep. 'Right…yes, I'll go.'

Her lips were tingling and her knees were weak. Perhaps an extra trip to the police station was her punishment for making such a fool of herself with Cristiano Andreotti, she thought crazily. How could he still live and breathe when she hated him with such venom? Or did she hate herself even more? How could she have sacrificed her pride for one kiss? Had stress deranged her wits? What vindictive fate had brought Cristiano back to her door when she was at her weakest?

In one harried step she reached the front door and yanked it wide. 'I have a pressing invitation to have another chat with the police, so you'll have to leave.'

'I've arranged for a glazier to replace the window,' Cristiano informed her.

Her teeth gritted. 'And why the heck would you have done that?'

'Isn't it fortunate that I did, when you have to go out again?' In a fluid gesture, Cristiano cast a business card down on the shelf to one side of her. 'My number…for when you come to your senses and accept the inevitable.'

'You are not an inevitable event in my life.'

Cristiano looked down at her from the vantage point of his superior height, his slumberous golden eyes glittering down towards hers in a collision course as keen as an arrow thudding into a target. 'Conversation is a much overrated pursuit between men and women. The kiss told me all I needed to know.'

Inwardly she shrank from that humiliating reminder. Her body had responded to him in blatant disregard of her entrenched dislike and defiance. But then how much would Cristiano Andreotti care about that? As he had just admitted, without an ounce of shame, he was more into the physical than the cerebral where women were concerned. She could not help but remember how she'd used to chatter on the phone to him. Had he been bored witless by the way she had rattled on?

While she wondered, Cristiano inclined his handsome dark head, strolled out, and swung into the limousine waiting for him. The long, opulent vehicle purred away from the kerb and disappeared from her view as if it and its owner had never been there.

Five minutes later a glazier arrived to replace the broken windowpane. All smiles, he told her that for what he was being paid he had been more than happy to give her job priority.

As she made her way to the police station that afternoon, Lydia was consumed by a helpless need to rerun Cristiano's visit in her mind over and over again. In a nutshell, he had offered to recompense the Happy Holidays charity in return for her sexual favours. Had he been acquainted with her abysmal lack of experience in that department, however, he might have been rather less keen, she thought ruefully. Yet she could not forget that eighteen months ago she had been so besotted with Cristiano that she had been on the very brink of being whatever he wanted her to be…

She was not proud of that weakness. But then she blamed her susceptibility on the fact that she had first seen Cristiano Andreotti in a glossy magazine spread when she was only fourteen years old. He had been twenty-two. Convinced that he was the most breathtakingly gorgeous guy she had ever seen, she had torn out his picture and kept it. She had not just stuck him in a drawer—no, she had ironed his paper image and put him in a photo frame, and spent seemingly infinite, essentially adolescent moments devouring his picture with wistful contentment. She had much preferred those dreams to the often crude reality of the young men she'd encountered.

In fact more than six years were to pass before she actually met Cristiano—years during which her popularity as a model had gradually brought her to the point where she had an occasional entry ticket into his rarefied world of wealth and privilege. Once she'd had the thrill of seeing him across a nightclub, lounging back like royalty and looking bored, while a bevy of women fought for his attention. He hadn't seen her or noticed her.

A frightening experience when she was only thirteen had made Lydia wary of men. After that she'd found it hard to flirt, and was careful not to bare too much flesh in mixed company. That she was still a virgin was a secret she'd kept very much to herself, for she had moved in circles where casual sex was considered the norm. She had also been endlessly hunted by rapacious men eager to bed her just so that they could add her to a macho tally of conquests. When she'd finally realised that she was being labelled frigid by the men she refused, she had been deeply hurt and embarrassed. It had seemed easier not to date at all. It had not occurred to her that her very unavailability might make her an even more tempting target for a predatory male.

The day she'd peered through the curtains at a Paris fashion show and seen Cristiano Andreotti seated in the very front row, she had been overwhelmed. The teenager who had once cherished his photo as a pin-up had surfaced inside her again. Edgy as a beginner on the runway, she had been afraid even to glance in his direction. In fact when he'd asked to be introduced to her, she'd been so sick with nerves that she hadn't dared to look directly at him. He had asked her for her phone number and she had told him that her mobile had been stolen. A moment later she had had to race off to do a private showing for a VIP. Later Cristiano had had a new phone delivered to her hotel, and his had been the first call, his rich dark drawl coiling round her like melting honey.

He had wanted to see her that night, but she'd had a booking back in London early the following day.

'I'll be in Sydney next week. Phone and say you're ill so that you can stay on in Paris,' he'd urged.

'I can't do that.'

'You can if you want to see me.'

'And if you want to see me you can wait,' she'd heard herself reply.

'Are you always this difficult?'

That had been her first—and not her last—taste of dealing with a very rich and powerful guy, accustomed to the instant gratification of his every expressed wish. Anything less than immediate acceptance or agreement was perceived as a negative response.

Even so, Cristiano had still flown her back to Paris the following evening to dine with him, and they had got on so well that they had still been talking in the early hours. Perfect white roses had awaited her when she returned to London, and he had called her every day for a week afterwards. She had felt cherished and appreciated. Every step of their relationship had struck her as being the very essence of romance. Plenty of people had warned her that Cristiano had a reputation for being notoriously cold-blooded when it came to her sex, but she'd paid no heed. She had ridden the crest of the wave of phone calls and all-too-brief meetings while secretly dreaming, as women had from time immemorial, of love and happily-ever-after. At no stage had it crossed her mind that she might simply be an object to be used and abused in a game being played by a super-rich, egotistical man.

Now, the pain of that final recollection did nothing to ease Lydia's tension as she found herself back in a police interview room.

The inspector gave her a surprisingly genial smile. 'Tell me about your mother's house in France,' he invited.

'France?' Lydia's astonishment was unhidden. 'But my mother doesn't have a house in France.'

'We believe that she does, and according to our source it's quite a luxurious second home. Five bedrooms and a pool, no less. At least, that is what she told a friend last year. That kind of set-up doesn't come cheap in the south of France.'

Lydia shook her head in urgent disagreement. 'The supposed friend is talking nonsense.'

'I don't think so…'

'Of course it's nonsense. If my mother owned another house, I'd have known about it. There's been a misunder-standing.' Of that fact Lydia had no doubt. After all, *had* there been a second property it would have been sold to ease her parent's cash-flow problems, and Virginia would never have made the appalling mistake of spending money that did not belong to her.

'We may not have established the location of that house yet, but we are well on our way to doing so. I think we'll have more answers when your mother is in a position to assist us with our enquiries.'

Lydia had lost colour. She was dismayed by the fact that the investigation now seemed to be changing course to place new emphasis on her mother's role. 'But I've told you before that she has nothing to do with this.'

'I believe that your mother has *everything* to do with this. You were unable to tell me what you had spent the missing money on.' The inspector settled a clutch of plastic evidence bags on the table between them. 'I have a series of cheques that were drawn on the charity account and signed by both you and your mother. One is made out for almost fifty thousand pounds and was used to purchase a four-wheel-drive vehicle. The salesman remembers the buyer well. Where is that vehicle now, Miss Powell?'

Lydia was aghast at the question. Virginia had changed her car before she disappeared? And for a larger, more expensive model? She was disconcerted by the information, but steady in her determination to protect the older woman from the consequences of her crime. 'I don't know…'

'All of the cheques we have retrieved so far relate solely to purchases made by Virginia Carlton, or payments made by her to settle personal debts. When did you sign those cheques?' the inspector queried, but did not wait for her to respond. 'It must've been difficult for you to deal with the day-to-day expenses of the charity fashion show when you and your mother lived so far apart. I gather the financial arrangements were left in her hands as she was on the spot. Did you pre-sign cheques for her convenience?'

'No—*she* did that for *me*,' Lydia insisted, a tad desperately.

The older man sighed. 'If you persist with this stance you will in all likelihood be charged with aiding and abetting your mother to defraud the Happy Holidays charity. All the current evidence, up to and including her careful disappearance, suggests that *she* was the prime instigator of the theft.'

'No—no, she wasn't!' Lydia exclaimed, her hands twisting together on her lap.

'And telling silly tales is unlikely to convince me, or any judge, to the contrary,' he spelt out impatiently. 'Stop wasting our time, Miss Powell. In due course your mother will be found and prosecuted. There is nothing you can do to alter that. I suggest that you go home now and think over your position very carefully.'

Lydia was on the brink of tears of frustration and fear when she left the police station. How could she have made such a mess of things? She had failed to convince the police that *she* was the culprit, and her mother was about to be hunted down to her hideaway—wherever that was— and dragged off to court regardless. Of only one thing was Lydia certain, and that was that her frightened parent could not *possibly* be hiding out in some palace with a pool on the French Riviera!

Although Lydia had been shattered when she'd realised what her mother had done, she had understood how desperate Virgina must have been. In the spring, Lydia had reluctantly agreed to lend her name to the charity fashion show that Virginia had set her heart on staging, and had contacted several other models. It had been around that time too that Dennis had cornered Lydia to ask her for money.

Lydia had been astonished, because her stepfather was well aware that the failure of the nightclub had left her penniless.

'But you know I don't have anything left.'

'Oh, come on. I wasn't born yesterday.' His heavy face had been taut with fake joviality. 'You must have at least one secret account—a cash reserve you keep quiet. Tell me about it—I won't let on to the tax man!'

Lydia raised a brow at such wishful thinking. 'If only…'

'I don't believe you…you've got to be holding out on me. I've been offered a terrific opportunity but I'm short of capital.'

'I'm sorry, I can't help.'

Angry resentment flashed in his pale blue eyes. 'Not even for your mother's sake?'

Lydia winced. 'I can't give you what I don't have.'

'Then isn't it about time you stopped playing at being a garden labourer and got back to the catwalk, where you belong?' Dennis demanded accusingly. 'You could cover the losses we made on the club in a couple of months!'

It had worried her that her stepfather should still be expecting her to provide him with cash when he should have been capable of earning his own healthy crust. It had not occurred to her, though, that anything could be seriously amiss. But, amidst conflicting stories from the Happy Holidays charity director about payments that hadn't arrived and a cheque that had bounced, and her mother's differing explanations for those same issues, Lydia had finally travelled to Cheltenham to visit. There she had been amazed to discover that Virginia had already sold the home that her daughter had purchased for her and moved into a hotel.

'What on earth's going on?' Lydia had asked, when her pretty blonde mother had opened the door of her hotel room. 'Why have you sold the house?'

The older woman treated her to an embittered appraisal.

'I can't believe you have the nerve to ask. After all, *you're* the one responsible for wrecking my marriage!'

Lydia gasped. 'How? What have I done?'

'You put my husband out of work. Now, not surprisingly—because we've had dreadful financial worries and I had to sell the house—Dennis has left me for another woman! Do you have any idea how I feel?'

Lydia experienced such a fierce jolt of sympathy for her deserted mother that she attempted to hug her.

'For goodness' sake, Lydia… Oh, all right.' Stiffly, Virginia submitted to being comforted.

'I'm so very sorry,' Lydia whispered with pained sincerity.

'Well, it's too late for sorry now, isn't it? If you'd gone back to modelling when we asked you, I'd still have a husband and a house I could afford to live in!'

Lydia felt horribly guilty—because she *had* put herself first when she'd refused to abandon her garden design course. Her heart ached for her mother, who adored her second husband. Having accepted Virginia's love and trust, Dennis had hurt and humiliated her. Lydia understood exactly how that felt, because it was barely eighteen months since she'd suffered the agony of a similar rejection at the hands of Cristiano. Fortunately for her, passionate love had turned to energising hate while she tormented herself for her own gullibility.

'What am I going to do?' Virginia suddenly sobbed. 'I'm so scared!'

For an instant Lydia was taken aback by the unfamiliar sight of her mother crying, but she was quick to offer reassurance. 'It's going to be all right. Whatever happens, I'm here, and together we can get through this.'

'But I'm in so much trouble,' the older woman had

confided tremulously, glancing up with a sidewise flicker of her eyes at her daughter. 'You have no idea how much…'

Her anxious thoughts sinking back to the present, Lydia walked home from the police station through the park. The steady rain would serve to conceal the tears on her cheeks, she thought wretchedly. She felt such a failure. She could not help Virginia if the police refused to believe her story. Why was it that she always ended up letting her mother down? And how many times had she already cost Virginia the man she loved? Had there been some curse put on her at birth?

First there had been Lydia's father, who would never have gone sailing in that wretched little boat had it not been for the pleas of his more adventurous daughter. It was true that it had been a terrible accident which nobody could have foreseen, but that did not alter the appalling consequences.

Then there had been Rick, Virginia's boyfriend when Lydia was a teenager. Lydia shuddered when she recalled the ugly ending of that relationship, and the bitter recriminations that had come her way. Whether she liked it or not, she had been the cause of that break-up too, and once again her mother had ended up heartbroken and alone.

With such a history behind them, Lydia had been delighted when Virginia had met Dennis Carlton and found happiness again. Although Lydia had disliked her stepfather, she had been content to pretend otherwise for her mother's sake. If only her mother had foreseen that in her desperation to keep her husband, and lessen the strain on their marriage, she would feel that her only option was to steal to pay the bills.

When Virginia had tearfully confessed the whole sorry tale, Lydia had immediately promised to protect her.

Virginia had been terrified, and so grateful. Recalling the rare warmth that her mother had shown her that day, Lydia felt her eyes overflow afresh. Virginia would never be able to cope with the shame of a legal trial or the rigours of prison life.

Overnight, however, it seemed that the balance of power had changed. Lydia's readiness to take the blame for the stolen cash was no longer enough to save her mother's skin. The police were intent on finding Virginia, and there was now only one way that Lydia could keep her pledge to get the older woman off the hook.

Soaked to the skin and numb with cold, Lydia leant back against the worn front door of her home and closed it behind her. She lifted Cristiano's business card. If he repaid the missing money, the charges would be dropped and her mother would be able to come home again. Virginia would be safe—and wasn't that all that truly mattered?

She chose to text rather than phone Cristiano, because she could not bear to make a surrender speech.

You've got me if you want me.

CHAPTER THREE

WITHIN minutes, Lydia's phone rang.

'Lia…' Cristiano murmured softly, sounding out and savouring every syllable.

'It's Lydia. Lia was the name the modelling agency insisted I use, and I never liked it,' she told him flatly, while her heart beat very fast somewhere in the region of her throat. 'I need you to pay back the money quickly, so that the charity will withdraw their charges. Can you do that?'

'It's not a problem. Are the police behind your sudden change of heart?'

'Does it matter?'

'No. Winning is all,' Cristiano conceded without hesitation. 'But we can't reach agreement before we've ironed out the finer details.'

Blinking back the hot tears of humiliation washing her eyes, Lydia clutched the phone as though she was hanging off the edge of a cliff. 'That's not what you said earlier today!'

'You should have been more receptive. The necessary formalities can be dealt with tomorrow. You'll have to come to London.'

'What formalities? Now you're making all sorts of conditions!' she condemned, threading shaking fingers through the hair tumbling over her damp brow. What on earth did he mean by *formalities*?

'Yes.'

'But it's not necessary. You can trust me,' she framed between clenched teeth, frightened that if he did not speedily repay the stolen money her mother would be tracked down and arrested.

At the other end of the phone, a sardonic smile of disbelief slowly curved Cristiano's mouth. She was priceless! This was the woman who, while staying below his roof as his latest squeeze, had eloped with another man. This was also the woman who stood accused of defrauding a charity of almost a quarter of a million pounds. Furthermore, loath as he was to recall the fact—for he was famous for his astute intelligence—when he had first known her he had actually been very impressed by that sweet-little-country-girl act of hers. She had been a natural at pretending to be what she was not. If he'd been a tree-hugging, weepy type of guy he would have got all choked up when she walked barefoot through the grass in his roof garden and confided that every day she was in the city she pined for the countryside. She was a real box of tricks, Cristiano reflected grimly.

'I'll arrange for you to be picked up and flown to London early tomorrow. Pack light. I'll be buying you new clothes. And lock up well and say your goodbyes locally,' Cristiano advised in the same even tone. 'If we achieve agreement, you won't be returning for some time.'

Bright blue eyes wide, Lydia shook her head. 'Whatever happens, I *have* to come back here. I rent this place. I'll need to sort that out, organise storage—'

'My staff will take care of the boring stuff for you.'

'But I have relatives here…and if I'm going away, I want to see them before I leave.'

'I'll give you one week after tomorrow, and that's it.'

Lydia sucked in a sustaining breath. The entire dialogue felt unreal to her. If she told him how much she hated him he would naturally want to know why. After all, on the face of it, she had walked out on him for another man. As far as Cristiano was concerned she had no particular reason to dislike him. He, on the other hand, would feel he had ample justification for despising her.

'I can't believe that this is what you want…you have to hate me,' Lydia reasoned tautly.

'How I feel is my business.'

His cool intonation made Lydia feel as cold as though a chip of ice had lodged in her tummy. She shivered in her damp clothes. He wanted revenge. What else could he want? When she had walked out of his superb country house with Mort Stevens, she had quite deliberately set out to make a fool of him. Now it seemed payback time had arrived.

At seven the next morning she was collected and driven to a private airfield several miles outside town. There she boarded a helicopter ornamented with the blue and gold logo of the Andreotti empire. A couple of hours later, she was being escorted from the helipad located on the roof of a contemporary glass and steel office block in London and ushered straight into a large empty office on its top floor. She smoothed down a ruck in the sleeve of the fitted black jacket she had teamed with a white T-shirt and a braided skirt.

'Mr Andreotti is in a meeting,' she was informed by a clean-cut young man in a business suit.

When his PA slipped back in with a shaken nod of confirmation, and rather pink about the ears, Cristiano knew Lydia had arrived and was exercising her usual stunning effect on the male sex. He was very busy. She would have to wait. Of course, she was only on time because he had had charge of her travelling arrangements, he mused, recalling how her unpunctuality had once infuriated him. He did not like to be kept waiting. Even on their first dinner date she had made a late showing. On arrival, however, she had electrified the restaurant with her beauty, approaching him with a wide, engaging smile of apology in a manner that had magically dispelled his exasperation.

In the act of listening to his whiz-kid executives trade facts and figures with a speed and precision which had never before failed to hold the attention of his mathematical mind, Cristiano found himself wondering what Lydia would be wearing. A split second later he sprang upright, called a break, and strode out of the boardroom into the adjoining office.

Sunlight glistening over her silvery fair hair, which she had confined with a clip, Lydia turned from the window that stretched the entire length of one wall. Her face, with its wide cheekbones and ripe pink mouth, was dominated by eyes as bright a blue as a midsummer sky. She focused on Cristiano's sudden entry, her heart thudding like crazy. Her tension rose as though a pressure gauge had been turned up too high. Beneath the current of apprehension lurked an edge of excitement that shocked her. When she had been seeing him, she had often found her responses to him so strong they scared her, and the reminder of that reality was unwelcome.

Sheathed in a stylish business suit that outlined his broad shoulders, narrow hips and long, lean legs in the finest mohair and silk blend wool, Cristiano looked spectacular. He was fantastically handsome, always superbly dressed and immaculate, always intimidating. His dark eyes glinted gold in the bright light. He really did have the most beautiful eyes, she acknowledged grudgingly, and a tiny pulse began to flicker below her collarbone.

The silence pounded and she couldn't bear it. Tossing back her head, so that a few silver-gilt strands of hair fell free of the clip, she lifted her chin. 'So here I am…as ordered.'

'Yes,' Cristiano rasped softly. 'It feels good to have you here.'

She had hoped to discomfit him with her comment, but he betrayed no unease whatsoever. Indeed, something in his rich, dark intonation sent the blood climbing below her fair skin. She had the horrendous suspicion that he was enjoying the situation. Furthermore, he was watching her with the incisive attention of a hunting hawk. When that narrowed golden gaze travelled over her, she was suddenly disturbingly aware of every pulse point in her body. Cupped in a fine cotton bra, her breasts stirred beneath her T-shirt, the tender peaks swelling.

'I can't believe you really mean to go through with this!' she told him breathlessly.

A sinfully attractive smile slashed his well-shaped masculine mouth. 'Every time I look at you I *know* I'm going to go through with it.'

'But it doesn't make sense—'

'Makes perfect sense to me, *bella mia*,' Cristiano confided. 'I want you—'

'But I don't want you, or this, and I can't pretend otherwise!' she blistered back at him.

His shimmering gaze intent, Cristiano strolled closer. 'If I believed that, you wouldn't be here.'

'B-believe it!' she snapped, infuriated by the way she tripped over the word, standing her ground with difficulty, for her every defence mechanism was trying to drive her into retreat.

'Since I'm the only rescue option you've got, shouldn't you be trying to persuade me that you're exactly what I want and need?'

He was so glaringly right on that score that she was seized by a combustible mix of fear and annoyance. He *was* her only hope. Suppose he took offence? Suppose he changed his mind? Where would her mother be then?

'Lydia…'

'What…?'

Cristiano was so close that she could have stretched out an arm and touched him, so close that she was alarmingly conscious of his sheer height and breadth. Her concentration was gone. There was the faintest tang of some exotic masculine cologne in the air and her heart was beating so fast she could hardly breathe.

Cristiano caught her to him with strong hands and drew her unresisting body into his arms. 'This is why you're being rescued,' he intoned huskily.

The most delicious tension tautened her every muscle. She knew it was wicked, but when she studied his lean, darkly handsome face, something wild leapt through her and made nonsense of her resistance. He curved long brown fingers to her cheekbone and let his hungry mouth taste hers with a sweet, savouring sensuality that tantalised her. The hand at her hip pressed her into the hard, muscular embrace of his powerful masculine frame, and she gasped beneath the probing exploration of his tongue. A dam of hot dark pleasure overflowed and roared through her in response. Suddenly her legs were like jelly and her breathing was rapid, and she was hanging on to him to stay upright.

Cristiano lifted her off her feet and brought her down on top of his desk. He meshed long fingers into the tumbling hair he had already released to tip her head back and allow him access to her throat. He covered her lowered eyelids, her cheeks, with tiny teasing kisses that made her want to curve round him like a sinuous cat, begging for more. He let his teeth graze her neck and he tasted her smooth white skin with lips and tongue, lingering in sensitive places, forcing a driven moan from her. Bending her back with astonishing ease over his arm, he pushed the T-shirt out of his path and glided his fingers up over her taut and quivering ribcage to curve his hand to a tiny pouting white breast. Her spine arched and she jerked as if she had been electrified. The brush of his thumb over the swollen and sensitive tip was a source of seething pleasure. The sound of her own choked cry of response catapulted her back to renewed awareness of her surroundings.

'For goodness' sake…*no!*' she gasped, pulling away and throwing herself off the desk in such a panic that she over-balanced and went down on her knees on the carpet. He stretched down a hand to help her rise again, but she scrambled up under her own steam and backed away fast. She was in as much shock as if she had been in an accident and her body felt heavy and clumsy and achingly disappointed.

'*Per meraviglia*…you could have broken your ankle.' Cristiano surveyed her with smouldering intensity and a frown of reproof.

Lydia was all the more shaken by the subtle shift in his manner. All of a sudden his tone was more intimate, possessive. He had kissed her and touched her, and she had encouraged him, and now he was telling her off.

Cristiano elevated a dark brow. 'Why are you so skittish? What's the deal? If the nervous virgin act is supposed to be sexy, it's not working, so you can drop it now.'

'I'm not putting on an act!' Shame and mortification blazed through her slender length like a burning flame. In her mind it was one thing to submit, but quite another to enjoy being touched by him to such an extent that she had had to knot her fingers into fists by her sides. Desire was in her like a cruel enemy, eager to betray her. And she could not win such a battle, nor even wish in the circumstances that she could. Suddenly she felt as trapped as if she had been put in a dungeon behind a solid steel door.

Pale as milk, she shot him an appalled glance from vivid blue eyes. 'I can't do this…I can't!'

Cursing himself for moving too fast, even while he wondered what had unnerved her to such an extent, Cristiano settled a chair down beside her as if she had not spoken and invited her to sit down. Unwittingly guided back into the safer tracks of polite behaviour, Lydia sank down, closing out her agitated thoughts in a desperate effort to regain her composure.

Cristiano handed her a document. 'This is the co-habitation agreement that I would like you to sign.'

Her smooth brow furrowed. 'It's a…what?'

'A co-habitation agreement. I haven't lived with a woman before, and there must be no misunderstanding with regard to the nature of our relationship. It merely defines our arrangement in the simplest terms possible and gives it a business rather than a personal basis,' Cristiano proffered smoothly. 'In it, the money which I am to repay the charity on your behalf becomes your fee for assuming the role of my hostess for the next year. You're lucky that I'm not including the donation I gave as part of that debt.'

Ludicrously unprepared for what he was telling her, Lydia nodded very slowly. 'Your…hostess?'

'A convenient label—'

Her eyes were widening and her sense of unreality was increasing. 'You're giving me an employment contract?'

His lean, strong face was sardonic. 'Nobody working for me earns that much.'

Lydia flushed red, then white, and focused carefully on the third button on his jacket. 'I'm agreeing of my own free will to all your demands…surely it's not necessary to tie me down to an actual written contract, with rules and conditions?'

'I believe that it is. Trust is a definite issue here.'

Her throat closed over, making her voice a little hoarse as she fought back angry tears. 'I think you're determined to make this entire affair as humiliating as you possibly can.'

'That's not the case. I think it's important that you know exactly where you stand with me,' Cristiano spelt out. 'If you break the agreement, you will have to pay back the money.'

Lydia was aghast at that information. 'But that would be impossible! Do you think I'd be here now if I had an alternative?'

'I know,' Cristiano confirmed without remorse. 'But I want to be assured of your loyalty.'

'My…loyalty?' she queried uncertainly, clutching the thick document while she strove to work out exactly what he meant.

His brooding dark eyes took on a derisive light. 'Your track record on that score is abysmal. Tell me, out of interest,' he murmured, 'were you shagging Mort Stevens the entire time I was seeing you?'

Feverish pink stained her porcelain-pale complexion. 'How can you ask me that? Of course I wasn't… I mean, nothing happened—'

'Even as a kid, I didn't go for fairy stories,' Cristiano sliced back very drily, his attention welded to the soft fullness of her lower lip. 'We need to move on—and fast. I have to get back to work.'

She bit her lip painfully at that tone of dismissal.

'I've made an appointment for you to see a solicitor so that you can enjoy independent legal advice,' Cristiano continued. 'If you decide to sign the contract, do so before three this afternoon. You'll then be returned to the airport for your journey home by private plane. A limo is waiting now to take you to the solicitor. Any questions?'

She was intimidated by his inhuman detachment. 'You said something about a year. Is that how long you expect this arrangement to last?'

Cristiano shrugged with fluid ease of movement. 'A day, a week, a month... A year is your limit, not mine. If you're still with me then, and I doubt it, you'll be free at the end of that period to renegotiate your terms.'

Lydia could not credit what she was hearing. Even the use of that horrible word 'renegotiate' demeaned her. Was his opinion of her so low that he assumed she was content to accept money in return for her sexual favours? But taking off with Mort Stevens had given him that impression, and she had only herself to blame for that. Her conscience reminded her that while that might be true, it was never too late to speak up and tell the truth—even if she was only prepared to offer a part of the truth. 'Can I say just one thing? And will you listen?'

Recognising that a last-minute plea was about to come his way, Cristiano hardened his heart against her deceptive appeal. With that gorgeous face and lithe, shapely body, she was every guy's fantasy, he acknowledged with bleak conviction. Add to that an air of vulnerability that implied she was a deeply sensitive soul and she became lethal. This time around, however, he had no intention of swallowing her sweet bait and being played for a fool.

He consulted his watch. 'You have one minute.'

'I just think I should warn you that I'm not what you think I am...' Yet, now that she had the opportunity she had sought, Lydia was having difficulty finding the right words. 'You're expecting a woman with a lot more know-how than me. I doubt that I can be what you want—'

'You'll be exactly what I want, because you don't have a choice. Don't embarrass me with this bull, *gioia mia*.' Cristiano sent her a winging glance of scornful amusement that rubbed her raw as an acid bath. 'Next you'll be fluttering those phenomenal eye lashes and swearing that you're a virgin, untouched by human hand!'

Lydia was rigid, her eyes as bright a blue as a peacock feather against the hectic flush that had climbed her cheeks as he spoke. 'And what if I was?'

Cristiano threw back his arrogant dark head and laughed with sardonic appreciation. 'I can safely promise you that if you turn out to be a virgin I'll marry you!'

'Is that a fact? Well, I wouldn't have you for a husband if you were the last man alive on this earth!' she bit out fiercely as she stalked to the door. 'Do you hear me?'

'Don't forget your deadline.'

While Lydia waited for the lift, she was conscious of being watched by a bunch of male executives chatting in the hall. Did others already suspect that she might be Cristiano Andreotti's latest acquisition? Her lovely face heated all over again, and a hard knot of chagrin and misery formed in her tummy. She had thrown proud words with no substance behind them, because he had made her feel such an idiot when he laughed at her, but of course he would never marry her or even offer to do so. Men didn't marry women they could buy or women they despised. Yet when she had been seeing him she had dreamt of the impossible, and that lowering memory hurt almost as much as his derision.

In the limo, Lydia studied the contract. Some of it she understood, but most of it she found impenetrable. He was determined to ensure that she depended on him for everything, from the roof over her head to the clothes on her body and the very food she ate. She shuddered with distaste. He would own her body and soul. She would have no rights left to exercise, for he would have taken them all away. She would simply be Cristiano Andreotti's whore. That was the price she was about to pay for trying to save face and hit back at him for breaking her heart.

'This is a legal work of art.' The urbane lawyer, an older man with shrewd eyes, tapped the agreement in wry acknowledgement. 'There's even a seven-point confidentiality clause which prevents you from talking about the contract or your relationship with Mr Andreotti outside this office.'

Lydia swallowed slowly. 'What's your opinion?'

'If you don't need the money, *run*,' he advised ruefully. 'There is no equality in this contract. While you are required to meet a strict code of conduct, Mr Andreotti can dispense with your services at any time and without explanation. Furthermore, neither your duties nor your hours of employment are defined. Sign and you will be contractually bound to agree to whatever Mr Andreotti demands.'

Lydia nodded heavily.

'Should you breach the contract, however, two hundred and fifty thousand pounds will immediately become a debt that requires repayment. That threat will put considerable pressure on you to meet all expectations, reasonable or otherwise.'

'I know,' she muttered tautly.

'Mr Andreotti is, however, disposed to be extremely generous in other ways. He promises to ensure that you enjoy every possible luxury and advantage while you remain with him.' His mouth quirked. 'He may be offering you modern-day slavery, but at least it's slavery with solid gold manacles.'

Having signed, she travelled to the airport. Already she was frantically trying to work out what she would tell Gwenna, for she could see no good reason to distress her cousin with the sordid truth.

Forty-eight hours later a removal firm arrived at her little terraced home to crate up her possessions. She had already given notice to the rental agency. The following day the police contacted her to say that the charges against her and her mother had been withdrawn. A tide of relief flooded Lydia, leaving her weak, and she wished that she had some way of contacting her mother to assure her that she was no longer at risk of arrest. Virginia had believed it would be safer if her daughter did not know how to get in touch with her, and had promised that she would phone when the fuss was all over. Lydia texted Gwenna to share her good news, and, as she had expected, her cousin called in on her way home from school.

'Why is a removal van sitting outside?' the brunette demanded, elevating a brow at the sight of the man engaged in packing china in the kitchen.

'Come upstairs,' Lydia urged.

'Are you moving somewhere?' Gwenna pressed worriedly.

'I'm moving out.' Lydia bent over the suitcase lying open on the bed to wedge a shoe in one corner. 'You remember I told you that I'd broken up with someone before I left London last year?'

'Well, you didn't spill many beans—only that the revolting rock star was a publicity stunt that went wrong,'

Gwenna reminded her wryly. 'You didn't tell me who the mysterious someone was.'

'Cristiano Andreotti…you probably haven't heard of him—'

'We do live on the same planet, and I read the same magazines you do. Did you really date that mega-rich womaniser? No wonder you got burned!'

Lydia mentally crossed her fingers, because she was about to lie. 'When Cristiano saw that story about the missing money in the paper, he came to see me. He wanted to help,' Lydia hurried on, determined to tell her story before she could be interrupted. 'He's paid back the money, the charges have been dropped and we're getting together again.'

Gwenna dealt her an astounded look. 'So that's why you want to return to London…'

'I'm moving in with him. No, don't say anything! I know you don't approve—'

'Of course I don't. What am I supposed to think? He stumps up two hundred and fifty grand and five minutes later you're agreeing to live with him?'

Lydia winced. She saw no point in upsetting her cousin with the truth, but it was not as easy as she had hoped to tell a convincing story. In desperation she reached for the old biscuit box by the bed, which contained keepsakes from her adolescence. Wrenching off its lid, she lifted out the photo that she was seeking.

'Who's that?' Gwenna questioned.

Her face uncomfortably hot, Lydia handed it over. 'I cut it out of a newspaper when I was fourteen.'

Gwenna fixed astonished eyes on her cousin. 'But this is him, isn't it? Cristiano Andreotti? You had a crush on him when you were that young?'

'Yes. He's the love of my life, and, to be frank, what he's offering me now is as good as it's likely to get,' Lydia contended tautly, accepting the return of the photo and thrusting it down on the windowsill as though the worn metal frame was red-hot. 'I really want to be with him. Please don't spoil it for me.'

Gwenna studied her unhappily, compressed her lips and said nothing more. Instead the cousins discussed practicalities, with Gwenna offering to receive and check Lydia's post.

A member of Cristiano's staff rang to inform Lydia of her travelling schedule for departure, and she wondered if Cristiano's use of a third party to pass on his orders was a taste of what life would be like with him. It made her feel very much like an employee. It also sent a shiver of apprehension travelling through her. What would her life be like with Cristiano running the whole show?

In actuality, her first destination in London turned out to be an exclusive beauty salon, where she discovered that she had been booked in for an incredible range of treatments. She found it humiliating that Cristiano was evidently not even prepared to see her until she had been groomed to within an inch of her life. The rest of the day passed while she moved from one room to the next, her skin glowing from a spa, a massage and a facial, her nails manicured, her mane of unruly waves conditioned and styled back into shape.

Cristiano phoned only when she was back in the limo that had come to collect her.

'Did you enjoy being pampered again?' His honeyed dark drawl skimmed down her spinal cord and she tensed and sat up, clutching the phone between taut fingers. His voice made her think about sex, and ensured that she was suddenly contemplating the shocking reality that she would be sharing a bed with him that night.

'Yes…yes, of course,' she fibbed, reasoning that there was no point in sharing her true feelings with him.

'I can't join you for dinner. Make yourself comfortable at the apartment,' he advised, breaking off momentarily to speak to someone and then returning to conclude the brief dialogue in a tone of preoccupation. 'I'll meet you at a club later.'

His apartment proved to be even vaster than she had appreciated on her only previous visit. A manservant, clearly following orders, showed her round a very long procession of cool, contemporary rooms hung with breathtaking art, before finally ushering her into a bedroom which mercifully bore no sign of male occupation. Lydia breathed again and walked across the floor to examine the sleek silver dress which awaited her there. A creation of the season's hottest designer, it was fashioned of fabric that shimmered when the light hit it. It would, however, be very short on her, Lydia acknowledged ruefully, because she had extremely long legs.

But what right did she have to protest? Hadn't she signed a contract in which she'd agreed to be treated more as an object than a person? Her body was Cristiano's sole source of interest, and, as such, was to be maintained and presented in a manner that pleased him. It was horribly humiliating.

That feeling of having lost control of her own life was heightened by the arrival of a make-up artist and a stylist, both of whom had been engaged to add the final polish to her appearance. It also meant that she had no time whatsoever in which to eat the evening meal she was offered.

A big bulky man climbed out of the limo and introduced himself as her security guard, Arnaldo. When the car drew up at an ultra-chic nightclub in Mayfair, it was Arnaldo who dealt with the bouncers barring entry to all but the chosen few. She was ushered past the long queue waiting hopefully and escorted to a private room. On the threshold, she was greeted by a familiar and unwelcome face.

'This is some comeback you're making, darling,' the stocky, powerfully built banker Philip Hazlett gibed, with a look that made her feel naked. 'You're looking very fit. I don't think I can blame Cristiano for succumbing to a rerun with you.'

Colouring, she said nothing. She had never liked Philip, but he was a childhood friend of Cristiano's, who had attended the same public school. Cristiano, surrounded by men wielding notebook computers and wearing anxious expressions, was talking on the phone. His arrogant dark head lifted as she came in. In a dark suit, striped shirt and blue silk tie, he was drop-dead gorgeous. She met glittering dark golden eyes, fringed by black lashes and semi-screened from her vision. Simultaneously all the oxygen in the atmosphere seemed to vanish, and she jerked to a sudden halt.

Cristiano allowed himself to stare. It was a given that all his male executives would gape at Lydia like schoolboys, he conceded, for she was dazzling. Her pale blonde hair tumbled in shining waves round her spectacularly beautiful face. A glistening swirl of silver fabric graced her delicate curves and skimmed her slender thighs. Desire took a rare back seat for Cristiano as he appreciated how revealing the dress was. Just as swiftly he noticed that he was not alone in relishing that view of her bare shoulders and back and her never-ending legs. He cursed his own lack of judgement, and the sensual line of his handsome mouth hardened when he noticed that Philip was guilty of ogling too. What had happened to respect for another man's woman?

Aggressive antennae bristling, he shot a knife-sharp glance of censure at the offending male and the guy paled.

Strolling forward, Cristiano curved an arm round Lydia and swept her straight back out of the room, his security men falling in behind him. She could sit by the dance floor and drink vintage champagne. That would keep her occupied and pretty much out of sight, for his table was in a private booth. He let his fingers dance down her spinal cord. Her skin felt like the softest silk. 'You look and feel sublime…'

The caressing brush of his hand sent a spasm of almost painful awareness reverberating through her slim length. Her breasts tingled, their delicate peaks tightening. The dark, hungry note in his accented drawl made her knees feel as bendy as twigs.

'If I wasn't in the middle of a deal that's hotting up, I'd take you home right now, *bambola poca*,' Cristiano breathed in husky addition.

All of a sudden Lydia's knees felt a little sturdier. It seemed that nothing had changed. Rich beyond avarice though he was, Cristiano still devoted his time and attention to getting richer, and the woman capable of distracting him from business and profit had yet to be born. He was a workaholic in denial.

'What did you call me?' she asked, seeking a translation as he settled her behind a table.

'Little doll…'

Her knees now felt like concrete, unassailably steady and dependable supports.

Cristiano skated a confident forefinger gently along the exposed expanse of her slim thigh and made her jump and shiver in startled response. 'That's what you remind me of in that dress. It's very, very sexy—but really not that appropriate in public.'

'You picked it,' Lydia pointed out between gritted teeth, only he didn't hear her.

As a brimming glass of champagne was poured for her, Cristiano vaulted back upright again.

'Where are you going?' she exclaimed, before she could think better of it.

'I can't make calls here…' Cristiano laughed, shrugging with the innate grace that accompanied all his movements and indicating the music. 'Enjoy yourself. I won't be long.'

'Don't worry about it…I'll soon find company!' Lydia heard herself declare.

His lean, darkly handsome face froze. 'Is that a joke?' he launched at her, loud enough for Arnaldo to frown in surprise from his position several feet away.

'I just meant…talking…dancing—'

'No, and no,' Cristiano riposted with icy force. 'No talking, no dancing, no flirting. One false move of that nature and you're in trouble. There will be no second chances. Don't let me catch you even *looking* at another guy!'

Astonished by that chilling warning, and the derision in his hard gaze, Lydia had to snatch in a sudden breath and hold it to keep her temper under control. Forced to breathe again or burst, she leant forward without conscious thought and said, 'You'd better tell Arnaldo to watch me!'

Cristiano sank back down beside her, his stunning gaze flashing flames of gold as he slowly and carefully laced long elegant fingers into the pale waves tumbling across her breast. 'Do you know what I really want to do now?' he murmured huskily. 'I want to take you back to the apartment, spread you across my bed and teach you some manners.'

Open-mouthed, she stared back at him, shock paralysing her while colour washed her cheeks. That graphic response ripped through her hurt pride and defiance to remind her of exactly what their relationship was.

Slowly, he got up again. She didn't watch him walk away. Thanks to that absurd fiasco with Mort Stevens, he honestly believed she couldn't be trusted around other men. In fact he thought she was a real *femme fatale*. Why wasn't she laughing at the idea?

Instead she drained her glass and grasped it again as soon as it was refilled. Fear of the unknown had seized her and she was fighting it off. *His bed?* Would he realise that she was totally inexperienced? She thought it unlikely. After all, he had dismissed her claim of innocence with contempt, and she had once read that most men couldn't tell the difference between a virgin and a sophisticate. Her chin came up, her fierce pride kicking in. Playing the *femme fatale* to the bitter end appealed to her. Surrendering to him would be a sacrifice, and she did not want a guy she hated to appreciate that. She wanted him to think that he couldn't get to her, that she didn't care what he did or how he behaved. Indifference would be her armour, she told herself feverishly.

Forty minutes later, Cristiano broke the habit of a lifetime and delegated his phone. He strode back to his table and sat down beside her. An arm anchored round her, he lounged back, tugging her into intimate connection with the long, powerful sprawl of his relaxed muscular body. Celebrity friends and acquaintances began to drift up, for he was always the centre of attention. Incredibly tense and nervous, Lydia avoided all eye contact. Cristiano inclined his handsome head in aloof acknowledgement, exchanged the occasional sally, but he made no attempt to introduce her to anyone. Nobody dared to breach his reserve.

'Why are you acting like I'm not here?'

'That you are with me is my business alone,' Cristiano asserted with immense cool, even while he wondered why she was so on edge.

'I hate being stared at,' she muttered, wondering if she had been recognised as the former model and thief exposed by the tabloids. She thought that it was unlikely, for she had never been half as famous as most of the people present. Even so, tension made her tremble against him like an animal being exhibited in a cage.

'Get used to it. You're beautiful enough to stop traffic and you're with me. Maintaining a low profile isn't an option.'

He had never remarked on her looks before, and before she could think better of it Lydia turned her head to whisper inquisitively, 'Do you really think I'm that beautiful?'

'Why else are you here?'

Her momentary pleasure evaporated at that caustic response and she shifted uncomfortably. 'Can't we dance or something?'

'I don't dance.'

An employee signalled him from the door of the private room and he released her and sprang up.

A bag of nerves without his presence, Lydia downed more champagne. He had bought her out of trouble on a whim—as an amusement, an ego trip. Now he was laying down rules much as he intended to lay her down. Angry rebellion snaked through her. She wasn't to dance or talk with anyone. He had stuck her in a booth and deserted her like an umbrella on a sunny day. But he had said nothing about her dancing on her own, had he? Why should she hide? Straightening her slim shoulders, she got up. Her head swam a little, and for a moment she had to clutch the table to steady herself. How much champagne had she drunk, for goodness' sake? Flinging her head back, she breathed in deep and headed out on to the floor.

Ten minutes later, Cristiano came to an arrested halt on his passage back to her side. His ebony brows drew together above incredulous dark eyes. Lydia was dancing alone and there was a spotlight on her. Lost in the music, she was spinning with her eyes closed, silver-gilt hair fanning out in a glittering curtain, her divine body twisting in time with the driving beat. She looked amazing. Every guy in the club was watching her with his tongue hanging out, and he didn't like it. He wanted to drag her off the floor and take her home, and that caveman instinct startled him.

When Lydia opened her eyes and saw him, her reaction was not at all what she had expected. Somehow the messy tangle of emotions he evoked coalesced inside her to produce a treacherous current of raw excitement. She had loved him once, a little inner voice whispered in persuasive reminder. Wouldn't it be wiser to make the best of a bad situation? In confusion she stilled, her body awash with physical awareness. The tiny snaking curl of heat tugging low in her pelvis made concentration well-nigh impossible.

Without even thinking about it, Cristiano strode on to the floor and claimed her, lean brown hands closing to the elegant curve of her hips to urge her momentarily close. Her head fell back, her full pink lips parting, excruciating tension gripping her. She wanted him to kiss her. Never in her whole life had she wanted anything as badly as she wanted that kiss. He flashed her a dangerous smile and freed her again in an effortless dance move that took her by surprise. Taut with disappointment, she mirrored his steps, but such precision demanded real effort from her, and she soon learned that her limbs were slow to do her bidding. In fact it was a relief when Cristiano finally closed a hand over hers to walk her off the floor.

'Time for us to leave, *bella mia*,' he murmured thickly, and her tummy gave a wild little flip of anticipation that destroyed her pride.

CHAPTER FOUR

STEPPING out into the cool night air made Lydia feel dizzy—and concealing that reality was a challenge. The barrage of cameras on the pavement outside the club provided a welcome distraction, and Cristiano's security team cleared a path to the limo.

Subsiding breathlessly into the opulent vehicle, Lydia focused on Cristiano. His lean, darkly handsome features were achingly familiar. He was still so gorgeous! A lump formed in her throat because, for the space of a heartbeat, she was the dreaming teenager who had fallen madly in love with his photograph. She felt incredibly emotional and wondered if the champagne was responsible, but her reasoning processes were too muzzy to think it through.

'I'm sorry about tonight… Socially, it was a washout,' Cristiano sighed, dense black lashes screening his gaze and then flicking up to add sizzle to his charismatic smile. 'But I now own a controlling percentage of IFS and I'm in the mood to celebrate.'

'IFS…how thrilling,' Lydia told him, without a clue what IFS was.

'You are more of a thrill.' Burnished golden eyes connected with hers. His aura of power had never been more in the ascendant, and the delicious tension she had experienced earlier that evening gripped her all over again. He closed a hand over hers and tugged her closer, turning her round to face him so that she was half-kneeling on the seat. Her heart felt as if it was beating at the base of her throat, and she was on such a high of expectation she could barely breathe.

He rested a fingertip on the pulse going crazy below her collarbone, moved on to smooth it over the pale alabaster expanse of her skin beneath. She quivered, her breasts lifting and stirring, the sensitive crowns pinching into painfully taut buds.

'I want you so much, *cara mia*,' he murmured in a dark deep voice full of intimate intent. 'But you know that. You've always known that.'

Her lashes dipped, her lovely face betraying no change of expression. She was accustomed to hiding her thoughts from others, fitting in for the sake of peace, soothing more demanding personalities. Briefly pain broke through the numbing effect of too much champagne. She had once naively believed that she meant more to him than her predecessors, and had soon discovered how very wrong she was.

'So secretive…' His dark drawl was one of silken censure.

Lydia snatched in a desperate breath to swell her lungs, loving his voice, revelling in his proximity, her mind controlled utterly by her physical senses. He cupped her cheekbone to hold her steady while he tasted her full pink mouth, using his tongue to dart a more erotic exploration between her readily parted lips. Primitive excitement roared through her. Her hands swept up to his shoulders to steady herself, and a split second later he tumbled her down into his lap to kiss her. Her eyes were starting to feel very heavy, and she left them closed.

'I'm so sleepy,' she shared when he pulled her back up into a sitting position as the limo had come to a halt.

Cristiano laughed huskily. 'Not tonight,' he teased, urging her to climb out of the car, for the door beside her had been opened without her noticing.

The combination of sudden movement and fresh air was too much for Lydia in the state she was in. Her legs crumpled and she had to seize the car door to stay upright. 'Oops!' she gasped.

Cristiano observed her across the roof of the car. 'Oops,' he said, very drily.

Mortification almost swallowed her alive, for, by the sound of it, he had guessed what was wrong with her. Inspiration struck her, however, when she glanced down and saw that the strap on her shoe had broken as she stumbled. Flipping off the high-heeled sandal, she dangled it by the busted strap and fought to speak with clarity. 'Lucky I didn't break an ankle!'

Cristiano ditched his icy demeanour and instead came to her assistance. 'Are you hurt?'

'I'll live,' she told him bravely, hobbling pitifully in the direction of the lift.

'I'm sorry…for a moment I thought you'd had too much to drink,' Cristiano admitted. 'Drunkenness offends me…'

Clutching the bar on the wall to stay steady, Lydia ducked her head down and nodded in vigorous agreement even while guilt assailed her. But it was true. She totally agreed with him. After all, she was not in the habit of over-indulging in alcohol, and there was no reason why he should ever find out if she was careful. It was a question of mind over matter, she told herself feverishly as they entered the huge hall of his apartment.

'Come here.' Cristiano turned her round in the circle of his arms.

Lydia almost rested her swimming head down on his shoulder. It took a mighty effort to resist the urge. 'I'll just go and…er…freshen up,' she framed carefully, plotting a line in the direction of the bedroom.

Freshen up into what? she wondered, striving to enter *femme-fatale* mode while smothering a huge yawn and swaying. Discarding her clothes, she trudged into the bathroom to remove her make-up. Every step was a terrible effort. She pulled down the white cotton wrap hanging on the back of the door and dug her arms clumsily into it. By that stage she was feeling so light-headed she was afraid she was going to faint. Absolutely miserable, and ashamed of her condition, she sank down on the floor, struggling to breathe in deep and get back in control of her own body again. She closed her eyes—just for a moment, she promised herself heavily…

Someone was talking in a foreign language and she frowned, reluctant to be dragged from sleep. Had that same someone shaken her shoulder? Or had that been part of a dream?

Her head was aching. Her lashes lifted on a sunlit room that made her blink. Even as her pupils adapted to the bright-ness she recognised that the huge contemporary bedroom was entirely strange to her. She jerked taut. Her head turned on the pillow to widen her field of vision and zeroed in on the male back view silhouetted against the window. Tall, broad of shoulder, narrow of hip, long powerful legs braced slightly apart in a typically masculine stance.

Shock grabbed her by the throat and shook her inside out, provoking a slight gasp from her lips. Cristiano, effortlessly stylish in a beautifully cut dark beige business suit, swung round to look at her. Still talking in liquid Italian on his phone, he strolled over to the bed and sank down beside her. With a disturbingly confident hand, he gently pushed her tumbled hair back from her cheekbone. She stopped breathing altogether, wildly aware that she was naked beneath the sheet.

This had to be his bedroom—the one room that had not been included on her official tour the day before, Lydia registered in a panic. She had slept with him and she didn't remember it! Shame and embarrassment and disorientation seized her all at once.

Flipping shut his phone, Cristiano surveyed her with steady incisive golden eyes.

'*Buon giorno, gioia mia,*' he drawled softly.

Her cheeks hot, Lydia made a strangled attempt to return the greeting.

'No...' With care Cristiano repeated the phrase, and urged her to try it again. He did not quit until she contrived to pronounce the unfamiliar syllables to his satisfaction. 'Excellent,' he pronounced with approval. 'I would like you to acquire the basics of my language, so I've arranged for you to have lessons in Italian.'

Although she was utterly taken aback by that announcement, she said nothing while her strained gaze sidled uneasily to the dented pillow beside her own, and her heartbeat raced at that confirmation of fact. She had definitely been with Cristiano all night, and she did not even recall getting into his bed, never mind what they had done there! She was appalled at the blankness of her memory, and deeply ashamed.

'Even this early in the day, you look enchanting.' Seemingly impervious to the tense atmosphere, Cristiano skimmed a lean brown forefinger along the soft rosy fullness of her lower lip with a devastating familiarity that sent little nervous tingles of heat zinging through Lydia's quivering length. 'I would very much like to get back into bed with you, but I have a meeting.'

Lydia nodded with as much natural cool as a robot. Wild horses could not have forced her to meet his gaze.

Cristiano pushed up her chin with his thumb, enforcing the eye contact that she would have denied him. A razor-edged smile tilted his beautifully shaped mouth. 'You were amazingly affectionate last night.'

Absorbing that assurance, Lydia flinched, her mind running riot on what she might have said or done. Oh, goodness, was it possible that she had told him she loved him, or something stupid like that? How could she tell what she might have said under the influence of too much alcohol? Suddenly she wanted to die a thousand deaths.

His stunning dark eyes looked down into hers, the fringe of his lush black lashes simply adding to their dramatic effect. 'I liked it…I liked it very much, *carissima*. I also particularly enjoyed the exotic dance you performed—'

Hauling herself up against the pillows, her shadowed blue eyes luminous as sapphires, Lydia gasped in horror. 'Exotic dance?'

Cristiano shook his handsome dark head slowly and sighed with regret. 'You don't remember anything, do you?'

She shook her head in stricken acknowledgement.

'So I could tell you whatever I liked and you would know no different,' Cristiano pointed out without pity. 'That is why a woman should never get that drunk and out of control.'

Her slender hands knotted into fierce fists and she swallowed convulsively. Her pride was stung almost beyond bearing, but logic made it impossible for her to argue with that statement.

'I was concerned about you last night. I ended up smashing down the bathroom door in your suite. There I found you passed out on the floor,' he revealed drily. 'I brought you back into my room only so that I could take care of you. Nothing of a sexual nature occurred between us. It offends me that you could have assumed otherwise. I like my partners fully awake and aware, not in an inebriated stupor.'

Pale as death, Lydia compressed her lips and focused on the bedspread with hot prickly eyes. She hated him for owning the moral high ground, for having done the right and decent thing. Even though she knew that it was irrational, that was how she felt. Even so, she knew that in the circumstances he had the right to criticise her behaviour. 'Okay…I was in the wrong. But I don't do stuff like that normally—'

'It was dangerous. Some guys would have taken advantage,' he spelt out. 'I didn't, and I wouldn't.'

'I get the message,' she said tightly.

'You have a wilful streak,' Cristiano told her huskily. 'It infuriates me, but it also gives me a kick.'

Lydia shot him a startled glance and hugged the sheet to her breasts, for there was a light in his gleaming gaze that made her staggeringly conscious of her lack of clothing. 'You said you had a meeting,' she reminded him in desperation.

Checking his Rolex, Cristiano frowned and vaulted upright. 'You also have a busy morning ahead.'

'I…do?'

'Don't worry about it. Your staff will keep you on target.'

'My staff?' she whispered incredulously.

'Arnaldo, your stylist… You've met some of your support staff already. You also have a very efficient PA to organise your appointments and remind you of them. I don't want you so busy that you can't devote your time to me,' Cristiano confided silkily. 'You're flying to Tuscany at ten. We'll be staying at my *palazzo* for a few days. I'll meet you there.'

'Oh…' was all she could say, belatedly grasping why he might wish her to acquire a working knowledge of Italian. Support staff? He had actually hired people on a day-to-day basis to look after her? She could hardly get her head round the idea.

'I have a small gift for you…' He set a slim, shallow jewel case down on her lap.

Dry-mouthed, she flipped up the lid on a breathtaking sapphire and diamond pendant. 'I can't accept something this valuable from you…'

'Of course you can.' Cristiano removed the necklace from the case, turned her round and pushed her hair gently out of his way so that he could attach the clasp.

The superb jewel was cold against the tender skin in the shallow valley between her breasts. She was maddeningly conscious of his appraisal.

'Yes, I like it…don't take it off, *gioia mia.*' He bent down and captured her mouth with a hungry masculine brevity that made her tremble, then he strode to the door.

Her face burning, she refused to look after him.

'By the way, I want you to see a dietician in Italy.'

Her head flew up, blue eyes bright. 'Will you stop ordering me around?' she launched furiously at him.

'Don't hold your breath. I'm a bossy guy.' In the face of her anger, Cristiano lifted and dropped a broad shoulder in a studied gesture of untarnished cool. 'I promised to take care of you and I will. You look too thin to be healthy, so at my request you will take professional advice.'

Ten minutes later, with a lump of impotent rage still sitting like a rock inside her, Lydia surveyed herself in the mirror in his magnificent bathroom. Too thin to be healthy? She had always been skinny as a rake. Perhaps he meant she was too thin to be tempting? She squinted down at her very small breasts and reddened. Was he hoping to fatten her up like a Christmas turkey? She touched the sapphire and diamond pendant gleaming at her throat with an unsteady hand. It was so beautiful, but he had made it feel like the luxury equivalent of a ball and chain. Wasn't owning her body and soul by contract enough for him? Perhaps he was scared she might forget the fact? It was time that she showed him that she could not be controlled in every way.

Later that morning, Lydia boarded Cristiano's private jet. To Arnaldo's dismay, his charge had attracted a most unwelcome degree of attention on their passage through the airport. The perilously high red stiletto boots were out of season, and extraordinarily conspicuous on Lydia's long stunning legs. Her low-slung denim skirt was so short and tight it was a challenge to walk in it, and her lime-green top exposed a slender midriff adorned with a colourful fake tattoo above her navel. The make-up artist had revelled in fulfilling that special request.

During the flight Lydia ate a meal and tried to watch a film, but she couldn't concentrate on anything. She couldn't wait for the moment when Cristiano would see her. In fact she just couldn't wait to see Cristiano again.

Although she had visited Rome twice before, when she was modelling, she had never moved beyond the city limits or had the chance to go sightseeing. As she was driven through the Tuscan countryside she was enchanted by the scenery. In the somnolent heat of afternoon, the rolling landscape of verdant hills studded with ancient earth-coloured buildings and olive groves was ravishingly beautiful.

The limousine turned into a drive shaded by a long procession of splendid arrow-shaped cypresses. She sat forward to get a better look at the house ahead. The *palazzo* was very grand and very large, and the sweep of gravelled carriageway up to the front doors was adorned by formal topiary and playing fountains. The building looked as though it had sat there for centuries.

Nerves formed a tight little knot in Lydia's tummy and she climbed out into the hot sunlight to walk towards the imposing entrance. She could already see Cristiano, pacing in the shadowed hall, and she found herself smiling. Then she saw that he was talking on the phone again and sudden fury ripped through her. She wanted to race up to him, snatch the phone and stamp on it until it smashed into a hundred broken pieces. Bemused and dismayed as she was by that strange prompting, she slowed her steps.

As she approached, Cristiano fell still and stared, his frown induced by the particularly frustrating discussion that was unfolding into his ear. His scorching golden eyes locked to her slender figure like a heat-seeking missile and raked over her fabulous face and the glorious curtain of her platinum fair hair. He inhaled before letting his deeply appreciative scrutiny travel further south, to absorb her tiny waist and her spectacular legs accentuated by the ridiculously sexy scarlet boots. It did briefly occur to him on some inattentive level that the outfit was a touch off the wall, but what she was wearing was a great deal less important to him than the explosive effect she was having on his hormones. Without a word he cut the call and switched off his phone.

Feeling ridiculously self-conscious for a woman who had set out to fight fire with a visual putdown calculated to cause annoyance and embarrassment, Lydia flung her head back. 'I bet you don't like seeing me dressed like this…'

'*Per meraviglia*…where did you get that idea?' Cristiano dragged his attention from the ripe rosy pout of her mouth to let his gaze roam down to her slim pale midriff, which he now realised was adorned by bright letters in script. She had a word etched on her skin? 'Is that a tattoo?'

Lydia perked up at the look of astonishment that had drawn his ebony brows together. 'Not quite your style?' she prompted, sweetly acidic.

Having got closer to check out his suspicions, and noted that the word was actually a name—and, moreover, his own—Cristiano surveyed her with sudden vibrant amusement. 'Sorry to disappoint you. You've got my name written on you, and I don't mind that at all. It's good joke, but it also appeals to the caveman in me, *gioia mia*.'

Lydia breathed in so deep she felt dizzy, but it was insufficient to contain her aggravation at this far from satisfactory response. 'I was trying to embarrass you…with this cheap outfit, with the stupid fake tattoo!'

Cristiano curved a light hand to her taut spine to walk her into the vast and magnificent hall. 'Obviously, your beauty outshone the trappings—'

'For goodness' sake, I'm dressed like a hooker!' she hissed at him.

'*Dio mio,* let's not make a production out of the fact that, in common with most of the male sex, I like looking at a woman in high heels and a short skirt—especially when she is *my* woman.' Laughter curled along the edges of every syllable Cristiano voiced in his rich dark drawl. 'Yes, I know. It's tacky, predictable, even sexist. But at least I'm honest about what I enjoy—'

'I don't want to hear any more!' Lydia sliced back at him between gritted teeth. It had been bad enough that he had not been discomfited by the challenging message writ large in her attire, but to suggest that her appearance was something in the nature of a sexual treat outraged her even more.

'At the same time I should mention that, while I'm happy for you to dress in this manner within the privacy of my home, I would prefer you not to be seen out in public in such provocative apparel.'

Lydia dealt him a seething glance. 'Why? Are you scared it might give the wrong impression?'

'No. I don't want anyone else enjoying the same view!'

'Watch out…you sound possessive! It doesn't go with the Mr Cool image!' Lydia slung, furious that he was refusing to take her seriously.

'I don't think so…' Glittering golden eyes assailed hers with an almost physical force that shook her. 'You might let someone else enjoy *more* than the view. You were quick enough to play the slut with Stevens!'

The silence hummed like a buzz saw. Lydia flinched back in consternation and hurt at that derisive crack, and then swung up her hand. He caught her wrist before the slap could connect, and held on fast to her when she tried to pull violently free of his hold. 'Let me go!' she gasped.

Cristiano expelled his breath in a hiss. 'Not until you calm down, *cara mia*. I was out of line. But didn't I finally give you what you wanted? A sincere and honest reaction?

Congratulations—it's been a long time since a woman made me lose my temper!'

Lydia stopped struggling and lost colour. She dropped her head, determined not to betray her conflicting feelings. Yet at last she had the proof that her supposed preference for Mort Stevens had got to Cristiano and drawn real blood. He was human, after all. And if he thought she was a slut, could she blame him? Hadn't she ended their former relationship in a very public manner calculated to cause offence and invite the attention of the newspapers? But he had deserved that rough treatment, Lydia reasoned fiercely. A guy who pursued a woman purely to score and win a loathsome bet laid with his equally hateful friends had no right to have his finer feelings considered. *What* finer feelings?

'I apologise,' Cristiano breathed in the rushing silence.

Lydia jerked up a slender shoulder and continued to study the worn marble beneath her feet. It was not enough. It might be his first apology, but she really would have liked him on his knees and begging; anything short of that could only be a disappointment.

'Next time I'll let you slap me,' Cristiano promised.

A reluctant gurgle of laughter was wrenched from Lydia and she glanced up, her anger draining away. 'I'd have liked that better,' she admitted. 'There are times you make me so mad I could scream. You're the only person who does that to me.'

They walked through the hall, which was furnished with huge gilded mirrors and marble statues. Cristiano directed her towards the double doors lying open at the foot. 'I never realised how fiery you were, *bella mia*.'

'Why should you have?' Lydia worked hard at keeping the edge of bitterness out of her voice. When she had been head over heels in love with him, she had been blissfully happy and had had no reason to fight with him. True, she had wished he would understand her reluctance to sleep with him after only a handful of meetings. But, all too well aware that many of her acquaintances engaged in sex on the first date, she had been reluctant to blame him for his lack of comprehension.

'Are you in the mood to choose a new wardrobe?' Cristiano enquired huskily.

'Sorry?'

In the huge elegant reception room, Cristiano settled her down on a sofa and nodded at the hovering manservant. 'That's what you're about to do. I thought you would enjoy being the client for a change.'

A door to the right opened, and his meaning was clarified by the entrance of a model wearing a houndstooth check coat which she slid back to display the silk dress beneath.

'I like that…' Cristiano confided.

'Stuffy,' Lydia told him, wrinkling her nose.

'Sometimes I entertain stuffy people and go to stuffy places—'

Lydia sighed. 'It's a shame you were never given a dress-up doll as a child.'

'What sort of a response is that from a woman who has my name written across her stomach?' he quipped.

'I should've known you'd make a meal of that.'

A brilliant smile slashed his lean bronzed features and her heart lurched from the surprise and effect of it. In the interim, he shed his jacket and tie and dropped down into the seat beside her. Sliding an arm below her spine, he eased her close to the long relaxed sprawl of his lean body. She stiffened, and then gave way, enjoying that physical closeness, refusing to think about the fact. Cappuccino coffee was served with tiny sweet biscuits that melted on her tongue, and the fashion show continued throughout.

'I've got to see you in that, *cara mia,*' Cristiano decreed when he saw a striking blue evening dress, and three out of the next four outfits elicited the same response from him.

His determination to buy her an extensive selection of designer garments, every one of which cost thousands of pounds, filled her with deep mortified unease.

'I can't feel comfortable at the idea of you buying me clothes,' she was finally moved to admit. 'I put all that stuff out of my life when I quit modelling.'

'Why?'

'It seemed so vain and meaningless. I was just a clothes horse. I donated all my party clothes to charity shops.'

'How very noble and self-denying. I wonder why you felt the need to shed the trappings of your former lifestyle so completely,' he mused softly above her head, and she coloured, knowing that he had to be thinking with scorn of the money he believed she had stolen. 'So you then donned a pair of Wellington boots and signed up for a gardening course. I'm afraid I don't see the attraction.'

'I like the knowledge that I'm creating something. I love working outdoors.'

Curling her even closer beneath one powerful arm, Cristiano murmured in a tone of unmistakable finality, 'But now you're with me.'

'Probably not for long, though,' she dared.

'Don't get your hopes up, *gioia mia.* The more you play it cool, the more I want you.'

Silence fell, and the procession of models continued. When the showing was over Cristiano curled her round to face him and bent his dark head to claim her sultry mouth in a slow-burning kiss that lit a flame deep down inside her. 'If you don't go and try on those clothes,' he breathed thickly, 'We'll end up making love here.'

Her pupils dilated, she stared up at him, mesmerised by the high-voltage charge of his sexuality. Finally, in an almost clumsy movement, she pulled away from him and left the room. What happened to her when he touched her? All the anger and the hatred ebbed and she felt dislocated from planet earth.

Two svelte women were waiting for her to choose from the garments hung in readiness for her appraisal, and then to help her to dress.

Her expression now reflecting the haughty indifference of a fashion model, she strolled back into Cristiano's presence wearing raspberry-coloured separates. In absolute silence he watched her every move, and she was maddeningly conscious of it. As she spun round to walk back past him, she was awesomely conscious of the piquant little frisson of pleasure that shivered through her when she felt the onslaught of his glittering eyes on her. It really shocked her that his desire should thrill her to such an extent. How could she enjoy that attention and yet complain about it? Yet as she modelled outfit after outfit she felt more and more like a wildly sexy lady, and it gave her confidence an incredible boost. It was as though they were engaged in a tantalising and very private game.

When she sashayed in, clad in a white organza dress, Cristiano sprang upright and strode towards her. 'The show's over, *cara mia*,' he breathed in a driven undertone, closing a lean brown hand over hers...

CHAPTER FIVE

CRISTIANO walked her straight out of the room and across the hall.

Lydia was disconcerted, for she had inhabited a dream-world of her own while she paraded back and forth in front of him. 'Okay… So…?'

Cristiano led her up the superb staircase. 'I've told my staff that we'll retain the clothes until tomorrow. You can make your choices then.'

Lydia hesitated. 'I have to get changed out of this.'

'No need. You look like a perfect madonna lily in white. I'll buy it.' As they reached the magnificent landing, Cristiano shot her a glance from heavily lidded dark golden eyes. 'I must confess that I've never been so excited by a woman…and we haven't even hit the bedroom yet.'

'Oh…' His words were a reality check, a wake-up call that catapulted her out of her pensive mood.

'But we're about to.' Scooping her up off her feet, laughing at her startled intake of breath, Cristiano swung her up into his arms with easy strength and strode into his bedroom with her. He could not remember when he had last experienced such intense arousal, and he was on a high. If this was a taste of how she could make him feel, she was worth her weight in gold and more. Lowering her with scrupulous care down on to his bed, he decided that he was very satisfied with the deal he had made.

Having let her shoes slide off in a rather awkward manoeuvre, Lydia sat up, hugging her knees.

Cristiano studied her while he unbuttoned his shirt. He liked the way the light from the window fell across her face. Her blue eyes were as luminous as stars against the pale purity of her skin. Even so, he frowned, because she looked so young. He assumed it was the effect of the white unadorned dress, but he had discovered an unexpected gap in his knowledge of her. 'What age are you?'

'Twenty-two.'

Cristiano was disconcerted, for it had never once occurred to him that she could be that much younger than he was.

'I know…' Lydia, grateful to have something safe to talk about, added in a rush, 'I look at least twenty-five. I don't know why. I've always looked older. When I was thirteen I could've passed for eighteen. I'll have to hope at some point that the clock starts running the other way.'

'What age were you when you became a model?'

'Fourteen…'

Long enough to acquire a deceptively mature air of sophistication, Cristiano reckoned wryly. But she could have been only months out of her teens when he had first met her in Paris. He almost winced, for she had been more of a girl than a woman. Rare misgivings stirred. Simultaneously his attention locked to her flawless oval face. It was very far from the first time that he had tried to pinpoint exactly what it was that made Lydia Powell so unforgettable. Her wide cheekbones? The clarity of her crystalline blue eyes? That ripe peach-soft mouth that opened with such delectable eagerness beneath his?

Just as swiftly, Cristiano wasn't thinking any more. He was reacting on a purely physical plane and moving back to the bed.

'I held you all last night in my arms and I couldn't touch you,' he told her hungrily as he came down beside her. 'Every time I moved away you sidled back, like a homing pigeon.'

Chagrined colour warmed her cheeks. Evidently he had not been joking earlier, when he had teased her about being amazingly affectionate the night before. 'That must have been a pain.'

'I had a cold shower in the middle of the night. I'm not used to them…except around you, *cara mia*,' he qualified with subdued mockery, tugging her round with great care so that she was facing away from him.

He ran down the zip on her dress. She felt the edges of the fabric part at her spine and she tensed, for she wasn't wearing a bra. He pressed his lips to the hollow in her slender shoulder and she shivered in response, not even noticing the instant when the sleeves of her dress slid down to her wrists. But her entire body jerked in sensual shock when he raised his hands to explore the pouting curves of her small breasts and their tender peaks. She shut her eyes tight and swallowed a startled gasp of response.

'Let me look at you…' Disentangling her from the organza still clinging to her hips, Cristiano lifted her back against the pillows and began to trace the pale delicate swells crowned by lush pink nipples with caressing fingers. 'You are so very beautiful.'

Lydia fought a self-conscious urge to cover herself. But tension was rippling through her in waves, and her hands coiled tight by her sides. She collided with smouldering golden eyes. Famed though he was for his cool reserve, he could not hide his desire. His hungry, masculine appraisal made an answering warmth pool in her belly. When he bent his arrogant dark head and captured a rosy distended bud, teasing and tasting with his tongue and his even white teeth, she trembled. She had not known she would be so sensitive there, and he knew exactly what he was doing. Her fingers delved into his black luxuriant hair and curled. A whimper of sound was impelled from her throat, and then another. Wonderful sensation seduced her, until she twisted and turned, desperate to sate the longing that he had awakened.

Cristiano lifted his head again, sensuous golden eyes inspecting her. He curved long lean fingers to her fine jawbone and held her fast while he kissed her with passionate thoroughness, ravishing the moist interior of her mouth with his tongue.

'I've waited an incredibly long time for you,' he confided in a roughened undertone.

'It didn't do you any harm.' Her response was breathless, abstracted, because even while she was fighting to hold back her response to him she was simultaneously angling her head to extend her long elegant neck for his attentions. When he pressed his lips with practised expertise to a pulse-point below one small ear, tiny unmistakable tremors raked her slender length.

'You want me,' he growled with unashamed satisfaction as he levered back from her to strip off his silk shirt.

'It's possible…' Her mouth was running dry. He looked all dominant male and impossibly sexy. Pure muscle rippled below his smooth bronzed skin, accentuating the solid wall of his chest and the hard contours of his flat abdomen. His athletic lifestyle was etched in the sleek, powerful lines of his magnificent body.

'I think it's a certainty, *gioia mia*.' As Cristiano vaulted off the bed to remove his trousers she was still watching him, as though a spell had been cast over her. Sleek black boxers delineated the noticeable thrust of his rampant arousal, and the heat of intense embarrassment and curiosity swept her from outside in.

Immediately Lydia averted her attention from him, terrified that her expression might somehow betray her as a fake in the *femme-fatale* stakes. If Cristiano was to guess that he was about to become the first man she had ever slept with he would surely think it was hilarious. Furthermore, he would also realise that her supposed fling with Mort Stevens had been one big, fat pretence!

'Why should you have a problem with wanting me?' Cristiano asked silkily, sinking back down on the bed and reaching for her, his every instinct challenged by the aura of constraint and distance that now enclosed her.

'I don't have a problem in that line.' And Lydia was determined that it should be that way, that she should accept what she could not change but somehow remain above it, detached and safe from experiencing any real feeling.

'Liar,' he whispered thickly against her full lower lip, piercing gold arrowing down into dense blue in resolute probing enquiry. 'You fight everything I make you feel. You always did.'

'It's called self-control, Cristiano.' But her voice was distinctly uneven, for she was in his arms, the quivering tips of her breasts grazed by the black curling hair that dusted his pectoral muscles. Her body was already betraying her wishes, as she was painfully aware of the wanton dampness between her thighs.

'Lose it for me…' He nipped at her full lower lip and let his tongue delve deep in her mouth in an erotic foray while he skimmed off her panties with sure hands.

She shivered as if she was in a snowstorm. 'I *can't*—'

'For me...yes, you can. And you will,' Cristiano intoned in husky disagreement. 'You'll enjoy what we share much more.'

Scrambling free from his loosened hold, Lydia slid into bed, tugging the sheet over her. She made no answer because she was intimidated by the subject.

At her sudden retreat, Cristiano elevated a sleek ebony brow. 'Are you cold?'

Pink flushing her lovely face, she jerked a shoulder.

A wicked grin curved his beautiful sensual mouth. 'You were such a tease downstairs.'

Affronted by that assurance, Lydia sat up again. 'I was *not* teasing you!'

Tossing back the sheet, Cristiano drew her to him with easy strength. 'Nobody ever did it better,' he intoned, surveying her with grudging appreciation. 'You have this touch-me-not look, and it drives me crazy. I can feel the cheeky invitation behind it—'

'I don't do cheeky—'

'But you *do* do passion,' he claimed, bending over her to lash a lush rosy nipple to straining prominence with his tongue, and lingering to punish her tender flesh with a carnal skill she could not resist.

Her spine arched and she shut her eyes tight. He explored the soft swell of her tummy, skimming through the pale curls that crowned her feminine mound to the damp swollen softness beneath. A whimper erupted from her when he found the most sensitive spot. When a tormentingly sweet surge of pleasure engulfed her she lifted against him in bemused surprise, the breath rasping in her throat. Sensation piled on sensation and she writhed, her hands smoothing and clutching at the satin hard strength of his shoulders and his back. Wanton heat burned through her nerve-endings, filling her with restive energy, and her longing rose to an intolerable pitch.

Cristiano spread her out beneath him, long brown fingers momentarily clinging to hers. 'You're as hot as I am…'

'Don't talk…' she urged, passion-glazed sapphire-blue eyes meeting his in a brief collision as she pushed her mouth almost blindly up to his, a shaft of inner fear making her avoid words that might be dangerous.

In answer Cristiano drove her reddened lips apart in an explosive kiss, his hands fiercely linked to hers above her head as he slid his lean hips between her parted thighs. She felt his hard sex brush her stomach with a sense of wonder. She wanted his weight on her. She wanted to be so close that she did not know where he began or she ended. She squirmed up to him, tilting in a desperate effort to ease the dull ache at the centre of her. She wanted everything, too much at once, and her frustration tortured her.

'Cristiano…' she gasped strickenly.

'You're amazing.' He released her hands to press her thighs back and plunge hotly into the slick wet heat of her.

The stab of pain that accompanied that passionate on-slaught provoked a cry from Lydia. Immediately Cristiano stilled. Torn from the hold of the sensual world he had in-troduced her to, Lydia looked up at him in mortified dis-may, for it had not once crossed her mind that any degree of discomfort would accompany her initiation.

His incisive dark golden eyes narrowed and slammed down into hers, to hold her suddenly evasive gaze fiercely entrapped. '*Accidenti!* I don't believe it…'

Severe embarrassment clawed at Lydia. He knew he had discovered her deepest secret and she could not bear it.

'You're a virgin... *Dio mio,* there has been no one else.' His shock unconcealed, Cristiano stared down at her and slowly shook his proud dark head. 'No—don't even think of trying to deny it, *gioia mia.*'

Lydia felt her skin prickle and flush pink, from her chest up over her throat to her face. Chagrin was eating her alive, but at the same time tiny sensual aftershocks were still gripping her—and not unpleasantly. Ready to do anything to escape dialogue on the subject of her total inexperience, she closed her eyes and shifted her hips experimentally. She felt amazing. He felt amazing. The pain was gone as though it had never been. On a level where neither pride nor conscience could influence her she was still shamefully eager to explore the pleasure that had beckoned only to be so cruelly snatched away.

'Be still...' Cristiano grated. 'I'm trying not to hurt you.'

She looked up at him from below her lashes, thinking how handsome his lean bronzed features were and how much she ached for him, hating that enslavement but equally trapped by it. 'You won't hurt me.'

'I already have.'

'But please don't stop.'

A sudden vibrant smile curved his sculpted mouth, and with a raw groan of capitulation he sank deeper into her yielding warmth. She caught her breath at the intensity of sensation and trembled. He lifted her to him and moved with fluid insistent rhythm. She gasped out loud, for it was bliss, sheer bliss, to every newly awakened sense. Her heartbeat raced, her excitement was unleashed and control abandoned. It was everything she had ever secretly dreamt of, and she cried out loud as the spiralling charge of dark sweet pleasure forced her to a wild summit of rapture.

Cocooned in the aftermath of that surfeit of physical pleasure, she felt joyful and amazingly alive. She inhaled the achingly familiar scent of his skin and smiled dizzily. He kissed her with languorous gentleness and she lay contented in the circle of his arms. She adored the silence, the intimate feel of his long, hot damp body entwined with hers. For the first time in many weeks she was at peace.

He freed her of his weight but continued to study her with intent golden eyes that revealed no trace of emotion. Likewise, his expression betrayed nothing of his thoughts. Yet the electric tension that had entered the atmosphere was a powerful indicator of his true frame of mind. Her relaxation and her mood took a swift downturn in response.

'It seems,' Cristiano drawled, his melodic Italian accent unusually thick, 'that we have a lot of talking to do, *cara mia*. I'm not very good at that with women. You'll have to make allowances. But I need a shower first.'

Lydia was as still as a statue in the giant bed. So that was sex, she thought, her strained eyes feeling prickly, her throat tight and dry. She had finally found out what all the fuss was about and had not even been disappointed, as she had vaguely expected. In fact just minutes ago, after their passion, she had been feeling incredibly happy. That lowering recollection made her squirm. Even the slightest movement made her aware of a host of little aches and tender places that she would sooner not have been reminded about. She had not expected the stab of pain that had betrayed her inexperience. She had been even less prepared for Cristiano to realise that she was a total fraud in the sexual sophisticate stakes. He had been astonished, but he had not laughed, she reminded herself dully. Was that a plus?

Her brow indented. What did it matter what *he* thought? Why was she even wasting time wondering what *he* might think? Of what interest or relevance was that to her? There was nothing personal in their arrangement. That horrible contract said all there was to say. There had been no need for Cristiano to warn her that he didn't make a habit of talking to the women in his life. His lawyers had created a fifty-page contract expressly to enable their fabulously wealthy client to avoid that challenging necessity. She was just bedroom entertainment, and if he was displeased by her sad lack of exciting expertise between the sheets he could dump her right now, no questions asked, no apologies required. Suddenly it was as though a giant black hole yawned beneath her feet.

No longer able to stand being still, she scrambled out of bed. Terribly aware of her nakedness, she wondered where her own clothes were. Stowed away by efficient staff in some other bedroom set aside for her use, she guessed. For it had been obvious back in London that Cristiano preferred to preserve his own space. Her eyes aching, she snatched up his shirt and pulled it on. She felt as if she was falling apart inside, and that maybe only her skin was still holding her together. She rolled up the sleeves once, twice, and noticed that her hands were shaking.

What was the matter with her? What the heck was the matter with her?

Couldn't she live with the fact that she had been born to be Cristiano Andreotti's whore? Hadn't she just willingly given him what she had so effortlessly denied other men? Desperate for fresh air, she opened the door on to the stone balcony beyond the windows.

Her memory was serving up an excruciatingly accurate

picture of her behaviour while she had modelled the clothes for Cristiano. She pressed her palms to her burning cheeks in an effort to cool them. He had called her a tease, and she might not like the label but he had been right on target with that charge. She had gloried in his attention and revelled in every minute of being watched by him. The suggestive buzz in the atmosphere had thrilled her to death.

But, in the aftermath, she felt sick with shame and bewilderment. With him she was another person—a woman she didn't know and didn't want to know. She didn't like the way she behaved with him. She hated Cristiano Andreotti, she absolutely hated him, but when she looked at him, when he touched her, when he smiled in a certain way, this horrible cringe-making weakness could still surface inside her. She had not known that sexual attraction could be so powerful that it would totally overwhelm her loathing for him. How could that happen? Especially when she knew exactly what sort of a guy he was. Arrogant, heartless, notorious for his lack of emotion. It took a real bastard to give a woman white roses with one hand while with the other he bet fifty grand with his friends on the certainty of bedding her!

Desperate to punish herself for her behaviour, Lydia made herself relive that moment over a year back, when she had appreciated that the guy she had fallen hopelessly in love with was an unspeakable four-letter-word in the truth, trust and decency stakes.

Her insistence on a separate bedroom that weekend at his country house had exasperated Cristiano. 'I'm not into celibacy, and I don't see sex as a reward you give me either. We're both adults,' he had told her with a silken derision that had cut her to ribbons. 'So perhaps you should think about whether or not you want to be with me.'

Had he known what it would do to her nerves when he said that? That threat had cast her into despair when she was already feeling unsure of herself. Going to bed with him had felt like an enormous step to her, and she had needed to believe that if she slept with him it would actually mean something to him. Although she'd been very much in love with Cristiano they had still only managed to get together five times in almost two months. He worked impossibly long hours, travelled the globe, and was a stranger to compromise. Accustomed to others eager to accommodate *his* needs and wishes, Cristiano had been inclined to blame her for the infrequency of their dates.

Even so, she had been terrified of losing him that weekend, and had soon crumbled beneath the pressure. At pathetic speed she had decided that it was time to shelve her sexual insecurities and misgivings and capitulate. Ready to share that change of heart with him, she'd tracked him down to the billiards room, where he'd been playing a game with his society friends. Knowing that he would hardly thank her for interrupting that all-male gathering, she'd been about to walk away again unseen when she'd heard her name mentioned.

'So, let's talk about Lia Powell,' she had heard Philip Hazlett suggest, and her tummy had lurched in dismay.

'What about her?' Cristiano countered calmly.

'Don't keep us in suspense. Here we are together again, and you can tell all—omitting no sordid detail. There's fifty grand riding on this, and it's not the money, it's the principle.'

'Yes. Has the icicle finally put out? I can't believe you've strung her along for two months for nothing!' another voice commented.

'The gossip says the frozen lady is besotted, so the odds are that Cristiano is already shagging her senseless.' Philip Hazlett had loosed a coarse laugh. 'Betting against the Andreotti ability to score even against such odds wasn't our cleverest move!'

That cruel hilarity echoing in her ears, Lydia ran. Her world of dreams was shattered. It was demeaning to accept that she had been on the very brink of winning his bet for him by sharing his bed that same night. At first she planned to confront him, but deeper reflection persuaded her that she wasn't tough enough to conceal how devastated she was. The discovery that she was the pitifully naive target of a sexual bet laid by rich bored men in need of amusement had almost destroyed her already fragile self-esteem.

Afraid that Cristiano might seek her out in her bedroom, she took refuge out in the stone summerhouse in the grounds while an endless party continued through the night in the huge house. It was there that Mort Stevens found her, red-eyed and wretched and cold, at four in the morning. He was amazingly kind and understanding.

'You want to save face, and I could do with some raunchy headlines to remind my fans that I'm not dead yet as a sex symbol,' Mort admitted cheerfully. 'So why don't we walk out of here together and enjoy the bloody big scandal it will create? It'll infuriate Andreotti…and what's more he's certain to lose his bet!'

She wanted so badly to hit back at Cristiano, and since he didn't given a damn about her, taking off with Mort was her only option. It also made it unnecessary for her to see Cristiano again.

Unhappily, Mort was arrested at the airport for possession of drugs, and she was arrested with him. Her most important client dropped her from their advertising campaign and the ironic rumour that Cristiano had dumped her for drug abuse began to do the rounds. By the time her name was finally cleared, her career was dead in the water and she was yesterday's news.

Drifting back to the present, Lydia shivered, a slim fragile figure sheathed in a blue silk shirt that acted as a wonderfully understated foil for her natural beauty. She should have learned her lesson then, she reflected painfully. When she tangled with Cristiano Andreotti she always got badly hurt…

CHAPTER SIX

IN THE shower, Cristiano punched the cold button and stoically withstood the icy jets pounding his hot damp skin. Raking wet black hair from his brow, he switched on the heat and leant back against the marble wall.

A virgin! She had told him so and he hadn't believed her, he conceded, his even white teeth gritting on that acknowledgement. Revenge had hit a roadblock, a tripwire that led straight to a stick of dynamite capable of blowing his whole life apart. He was in deep shock. Even while he looked for someone to blame he knew that his own bone-deep aggression and arrogance had brought him down. And just when everything had seemed so perfect that he could taste it. For she challenged and amused him in a way that no other woman had ever contrived to do.

It should have been ideal—a relationship with a business basis that was on his terms. Black and white, simple and straightforward, with no room for misunderstandings or emotional scenes. He had liked that. He had really liked that. It hadn't mattered that she was mercenary and untrustworthy. A hunger for money had been the fatal flaw that had led to her downfall, and with the background he came from he understood avarice better than most. He had been happy to feed her addiction with money and jewellery and luxury beyond her wildest dreams. He had learnt very young what women expected from him. But now all bets were off on every score, because Lydia Powell was not the woman he had believed she was. How could she be? His image of her had been turned on its head and blurred out of recognition by one inescapable truth…

Eighteen months ago, without the slightest suspicion of the fact, he had been trying to railroad a virgin into his bed. Women had always eased his hunger so readily, so immediately, that he had been impatient at her reluctance. He grimaced. It was not a pretty picture. But even less could he comprehend her dawn elopement with Mort Stevens. Unless, he mused, he put those two facts together and read the message that had escaped him at the time, when he had still lacked the most important piece of the puzzle. *Per Dio,* how could he have been so slow to make the obvious connection that he now saw? A rush of rare anger energised Cristiano, and he snatched up a towel.

Lydia gave a nervous jerk when Cristiano reappeared in the bedroom. His black hair was still spattered with crystalline drops of water. He had paused only long enough to pull on jeans and a black shirt which hung unbuttoned to reveal a hair-roughened brown wedge of lean muscular chest. She had never seen him so casually dressed before, and it unsettled her.

'I've finally worked out what you were up to eighteen months ago,' Cristiano delivered with icy clarity.

A bemused expression stamped her lovely face, and she threaded an uncertain hand through the pale tangle of blonde waves tumbling across her brow, her frown deepening. His reference to the time when they had been dating completely disconcerted her. 'What I was…*up to*? I don't understand.'

Diamond-hard dark eyes gleamed with scorn. 'You were upping the ante. You decided to play a stupid childish game with me, and if you got badly burned you have only yourself to blame for it!'

Her soft full mouth fell wide. 'What on earth are you talking about?'

'Your sudden extraordinary flit from my country home with that ancient creaking rock legend Mort Stevens!' Cristiano derided with a sardonic smile. 'Obviously you were trying to make me jealous.'

Hot chagrined colour flushing her creamy complexion, Lydia went rigid, angry astonishment holding her still. 'I don't believe I'm hearing this. Trying to make you jealous?' she repeated with ringing distaste. 'Where do you get that crazy idea from?'

'It's the only explanation that makes sense—'

'Well, it's the wrong one!'

'Dio mio, what else could you have been doing with him? I now know that you didn't sleep with Stevens. There *was* no secret affair. The entire exercise was a manipulative infantile ploy.'

Lydia was getting so mad that she could hardly think straight. 'There is such a thing as an affair without sex!' she launched back, determined not to back down and admit that he had guessed any part of the truth.

'Is there?' Cristiano vented a caustic laugh of disagreement. 'It was all a fake. You holed up in his apartment for a few hours and then he took you to the airport to see him off and to introduce you to the press as his future fiancée. It was to boost his image and his album sales. It's so obvious now. I don't know why I didn't see it at the time—'

'You didn't see it because that's not how it was!'

'At one in the morning you rang my mobile, hung up before I could answer and switched off your own phone,' Cristiano recalled. 'That was your opening move and it was supposed to bring me to you. When it didn't, you had a note delivered to me saying that as things didn't appear to be shaping up between us you thought it was time for you to move on. That was the real bait—your threat to walk out of my house, my moment to appreciate that I was losing you—'

'You had *already* lost me!' Her luminous blue eyes were bright with fury at his scathing recital of events that night. 'And I did *not* have the note delivered to you. I left it sitting in my room.'

Cristiano looked unimpressed. 'You were still in the house when that note was delivered—but I don't react to that kind of pressure. I decided that if you were that keen to go home and sulk, I would let you do it.'

Loathing leapt up so high inside Lydia she was dimly surprised that she did not burst into spontaneous flames. 'So far you have called me stupid, childish and manipulative—'

'*Si, bella mia.* I'm being very restrained in my choice of words.' As Cristiano spoke, he was watching the sunlight lend translucence to his shirt and reveal the provocative outline of her delicate rose-coloured areolae. Almost imperceptibly he tensed, striving to cool the instinctive surge of desire that she aroused. 'Perhaps that's because in retrospect there is something rather pathetic about the little charade you were so determined to play out for my benefit.'

Her hands planted on her slim hips, Lydia slung him an

irate glance. 'Listen to me—there was no charade, no attempt to make you jealous!'

Cristiano groaned out loud. 'Mort used you for a publicity stunt, and you used him to try and wind me up into offering more than a casual fling. Do you really think you're the only woman ever to try that on me? Of course I was supposed to chase after you and snatch you back out of his wizened old arms, wasn't I?'

Her face burning hotter than hellfire, Lydia snatched up a silver-backed hairbrush lying on the dresser and flung at him. 'He's a much nicer guy than you are!'

Cristiano sidestepped the flying missile with offensive cool. 'But it's me you shagged.'

'Because—'

Glittering dark golden eyes pinned to her, Cristiano took a step closer. He just wanted to drag her into his arms and sink deep into her beautiful pale body again. He had never been so hot for a woman. '*Because*...you want me.'

'Because we have a contract,' she hissed back, colliding with his smouldering gaze. Her heartbeat started to race.

'The enthusiasm with which you're fulfilling my expectations is almost more than I dared to hope for, *gioia mia*,' Cristiano murmured huskily.

He was so close she trembled, and she attempted to break the spell with words, wanting to fight with him to keep temptation at bay. 'Why can't you appreciate how much I hate you?'

Cristiano closed long fingers to her elbows and drew her up against him. She jerked taut, but her eyes were as radiant as stars. As his hand splayed to her hip, to gather her closer, he could feel the tiny little vibrations passing through her slight figure and it gave him a high. 'Hatred could never taste as sweet as this…' he swore, and he crushed her soft pink mouth under his.

Without hesitation he stooped to curve a powerful arm below her hips and swept her up into his arms to carry her back to the bed.

'We can't… I'm not speaking to you!' Lydia protested frantically when he let her come up for air again.

'So?' Cristiano swooped down on the fingers she had raised in uncertain protest, engulfed them in his mouth and laved them with his tongue.

A frisson of heat twisted low in her pelvis, her tummy muscles tensing in response. She snatched in air audibly and the silence pounded. Her body was deliciously poised on the edge of wild anticipation. 'Don't…'

'But you like it, *cara mia.*' he breathed softly, his intent gaze narrowed to gleaming chips of sinful gold below ebony lashes.

Her very bones were ready to melt into the mattress beneath her. She studied him, helplessly admiring the strong slash of his nose, the smooth hard masculine planes of his lean strong face, and the beautiful passionate curve of his sensual lips. He was breathtaking. In a sudden movement that seemed to her to be quite unrelated to any process of thought on her part, her fingers slid from his shoulder up into the springy depths of his black hair.

'I don't like you…I really don't like you,' she whispered shakily. 'But somehow I find you…'

His shimmering gaze entrapped hers. 'The word you're searching for is…irresistible.'

'Dream on…' But the stormy hunger assailing her made her tug him down to her level so that she could claim his mouth for herself.

Breathing raggedly, Cristiano leant back from her to rip off his shirt and dispose of his jeans. There was nothing cool or practised about that process. She spread her fingers on the warm bronzed expanse of his chest, let her hand sink lower to the taut musculature of his abdomen, felt him shudder beneath her touch. She looked up at him in surprise. His eyes devoured her. In an almost clumsy gesture he cupped her face and kissed her with a breathless driving desire that sent a liquid tightening sensation shimmying through her.

'You burn me alive, *cara mia*,' he confided, unbuttoning the shirt she wore with scant ceremony, bending over her with predatory intent etched in every line of his magnificent length.

She trembled, and her eyes slid dreamily closed in silent welcome. He kneaded the lush distended buds of her nipples with skilful fingers and her spine arched, She moaned low in her throat. All thought had gone, to be replaced by a fiery elemental need that she was no longer able to fight.

'The very scent of your skin tells me that you belong to me,' Cristiano breathed erotically against her throat, when her entire body was taut and thrumming like a piano played by a master.

She shifted against him, thighs parting for him, the hunger already too great to be denied. 'Cristiano…'

He traced the damp delicate softness below her mound and she gasped and writhed, tiny cries escaping her, muffled in his strong shoulder as he toyed with the most sensitive spot of all. The pleasure was so intense she couldn't bear it. He came over her and she arched up to him, urging him on, frantic and out of control, wanting, needing, striving with every fibre of her being to sate her own longing for him.

'*Dio mio*…you match my passion.' One hand knotting into her tumbled silvery fair hair, he kissed her with sensual savagery. He slid provocatively against the moist heart of her, teasing her with the hot hard shaft of his sex. Sizzling golden eyes held hers with fierce desire. 'I like the fact that I am the first, the *only* lover you have ever had. I was shocked, but it is the most erotic discovery I have ever made, *carissima*.'

She said nothing, for she was beyond words, her whole being centred on sensation. He entered her in a single deep thrust and she cried out in urgent response. There was nothing for her but him and what he was making her feel. He had taught her this raw, insistent need that had driven her past the boundaries of control. He slammed into her faster and faster. Wildly excited, she moved against him in a frenzy of abandonment, grasping for the ecstasy she could sense lying just out of reach. In an instant she went from torment to a crescendo of glorious pleasure and plunged over the edge, quivering in shock as the ripples of ecstasy continued to tug at her. Nothing had ever been that intense for her. As he groaned and shuddered in satisfaction, her eyes were overflowing with tears. Dizzy with warmth and delight, she lay there, just holding him to her.

Perhaps it was unfortunate that just at that instant she should have caught an accidental glimpse of herself in the tall looking-glass on the wall by the door. She was wrapped round him like an adoring lover. She blinked and then stared, the mists of passion and misplaced affection dissipating faster than the speed of light. *Slut*, she mouthed at her image, hating herself with all the strength of character she possessed. At that same moment she recalled his last words on the score of her virginity, and such a flood of self-loathing filled her that she was surprised that her temper did not erupt like a volcano.

Cristiano lifted his dishevelled dark head to look down at her. 'That was amazing, astonishing…' He touched a wondering fingertip to the moisture sparkling on her cheeks and let his handsome mouth glide over her damp skin in a caressing benediction. 'We have something special here.'

'Time will tell. I was thinking about something else,' she admitted in a soft tone that gave no hint of what was to come. 'Isn't it a shame that you didn't know I was a virgin when you laid that bet with your friends?'

Stunned by the pure shock value of that controversial question, Cristiano jerked taut and rolled back from her.

Smiling stonily, she continued, 'After all, if you'd known that your target was a virgin, I imagine the stakes would have been even higher.'

For a timeless moment Cristiano shut his eyes and thought of every swear word he had ever known. That pointless pursuit was followed by a ferocious desire to smash his fist into the wall.

'Don't even *think* about denying it,' she warned him.

Brilliant dark golden eyes met hers with a lack of expression that infuriated Lydia. She wanted blood, and she wanted to discomfit and embarrass him. 'Your sense of timing is an art form,' he told her flatly.

'Is that all you've got to say?' Lydia gasped as he sprang out of bed.

'When…*how* did you find out?' he breathed, hauling on his boxers.

She sat up in bed. 'The party at your house.'

'That last night we were together?' he shot at her in astonishment.

'I went looking for you. You were playing billiards and the door wasn't shut. I heard you and Philip and some other guy talking,' she recited, bitter anger beginning to rise in her as she recalled that painful experience.

He pulled up his jeans. 'You were listening outside the door?'

'It was an accident!' she slung at him.

'And I never saw you again until I went looking for you last week,' Cristiano mused, darker colour demarcating his fabulous cheekbones.

'Are you surprised?' Lydia flung bitterly.

'No…' In an uneasy movement, he raked long brown fingers through his black cropped hair. 'But if you listened, surely you heard me offering to pay up because I wanted out of the bet?'

'Did you?' Lydia lifted and dropped a slight shoulder in dismissal of that plea. 'Really? Why would you have done that? And—even if you did—well, I'd evidently walked off by that stage, and didn't hear you say it.'

Cristiano expelled his breath on a hiss. 'I don't expect you to understand this—'

'Why? Why wouldn't I understand?'

'Because you're a woman,' Cristiano growled. 'That asinine bet was suggested a few hours after I was seen talking to you in Paris. It was the day we first met—'

'Gosh, that's so romantic,' Lydia told him, listening with an earnest air, her arms clasped round her raised knees.

Her sarcasm made Cristiano throw up his hands in a gesture of rueful acceptance. It was very charming, beautifully executed, and the effect was enhanced rather than spoilt by the fact that he was barefoot and bare-chested, with his jeans still unzipped. 'I had had too much to drink…we all had. I should have said no then.'

She tilted her head to one side, wildly tousled platinum-pale waves tumbling back from her pink cheeks. 'To me… or the bet?'

'The bet…*naturalamente*,' Cristiano declared. 'But a guy doesn't say no to something like that. It's all to do with—'

'Being a cool macho bastard who keeps his brains in his boxers?' Lydia asked bitterly. 'Don't you dare try to make excuses! It was disgusting—'

His strong shadowed jawline clenched. 'I know it was, and it wasn't my style, believe me.'

Her look was disbelieving.

'I didn't see those guys again until the weekend party at my house. By then I had forgotten all about the stupid bet. When the issue was raised—'

'Listen, don't use nice, clean businesslike words like "issue" to describe what I overheard. I heard those men talking about me in a manner that you should have objected to!'

'I *did* object…why did you have to walk away before you heard me doing exactly that?' Cristiano demanded in a driven undertone, a raw light in his dark golden eyes that lent them an unusual degree of clarity. 'Philip was drunk. I stopped the locker room discussion and I dropped the bet.'

The silence lingered while she considered that explanation. She had never known him to lie. Did he deserve the benefit of the doubt? Although she did not wish to give it to him, his patent sincerity was his most convincing defence.

'Will you accept that?' Cristiano prompted.

Lydia gave him a grudging nod, for she had enjoyed his discomfiture, that rare chance to see him shorn of a little of his glossy patina of aloof indifference. 'But don't ever expect me to forgive you for it,' she warned him.

'The bet is why you took off with Mort Stevens, isn't it?'

Again, Lydia nodded in confirmation.

'Why am I only finding out about this now? Why the hell didn't you talk to me about this when it happened?' Cristiano shot at her with a suddenness that disconcerted her.

'Why would I have?' she flung back at him, anger licking at her afresh. 'We'd only had a few dates, and it wasn't going very well for us that particular day, was it?'

'I had no idea you were a virgin. If I had known you were that inexperienced, if I had had the slightest suspicion, I would have had a totally different attitude. You should have told me.'

'It's so easy for you to say all this stuff now!' she condemned. 'Have you any idea how I felt after I found out about that bet?'

Cristiano tensed. 'I can imagine.'

'How could you possibly? I felt betrayed and humiliated. It was obvious that you were only with me because of a horrible bet, and that all you were interested in was sex.'

Cristiano sank down on the edge of the bed. 'It wasn't like that…'

'How was it?' she challenged.

The silence pulsed with undertones.

His lean, darkly handsome features were taut, his glittering gaze hooded. 'It's insane for you to believe that I was only with you because of a bet. That I utterly refute. I saw you; I wanted to get to know you. There was a very strong sexual attraction and I'm not ashamed to acknowledge that. The bet was a piece of foolishness between young men, all of whom should have known better. It was inexcusable and offensive and I apologise without reserve.'

'Yeah…right.' Lydia was lacing and relacing the fingers she had clasped round her knees. He had not denied her contention that his sole motivation had been sex, and that hurt. She questioned her own over-sensitivity. So she had loved and he had lusted? So it had been since time began. It was not the stuff of Greek tragedy, so why did she feel as though it was? Hadn't she always known that she was just another in a long line of fanciable bed partners in his fast-moving life?

In an unexpected move that disconcerted her, Cristiano tried to tug her back into his arms. Her emotions were already very shaken up, and in the grip of that inner turmoil she felt neither gracious nor forgiving. In fact, when she realised that he was attempting to assume a comforting role, her pride rebelled furiously. Rejecting him with positive violence, and pushing him away, she retreated to the far side of the bed. 'Leave me alone!'

Cristiano vaulted back upright and spread fluid brown hands in an angrily defensive gesture. '*Per meraviglia*…I only wanted to hold you. That, at least, should not be treated like a crime.'

Her head was beginning to pound with tension, and she felt incredibly tired and sorry for herself. 'That depends on your outlook. Now, I want to get up and have a shower in a room of my own—but I don't know where that is yet. And I want clothes…but I don't have any within reach. I also want something to eat!' To her dismay her voice emerged with a shrill sharp edge that made her want to wince.

Cristiano strode across the room and cast open a door in the wall. 'Your suite is through here. I'll get you something to wear…'

Her eyes felt horribly hot and scratchy, and she bowed her weary head. She had never felt more alone in her life.

Cristiano returned and laid her shabby pale pink cotton wrap at her feet. He maintained a careful distance, as though she had an exclusion zone marked around her. A huge lump mushroomed in her throat. She fumbled her way into the wrap, shying away from his silent offer of assistance. Like a snail bereft of its shell, she wanted to retreat into hiding—fast. Sliding out of bed, she went rigid when she brushed against him.

Her blue eyes glimmered with a determined flame, for she felt weak but had no intention of parading that fact. 'So, now you know I wasn't trying to make you jealous when I walked out with Mort that weekend.'

'And that maybe you weren't exaggerating when you said you hated me,' Cristiano incised, without any expression at all.

'That hasn't bothered you too much up to now. Let's face it,' she sniped, hearing the tart words flowing from her own lips and disliking them, but quite unable to stop them leaping off her tongue, 'you're not exactly Mr Sensitive.'

Cristiano watched the door shut. He didn't like that door closed between them. He swore vehemently under his breath. A gigantic wave of unfamiliar frustration gripped him. He was in shock. He wasn't used to being taken by surprise or put in the wrong. It was unnerving to suffer that experience twice in the same day. But much that had been obscure was now crystal-clear. She had an exquisite grasp of the concept of revenge. Mort Stevens had been a reprisal attack, a direct hit. To accept that he owed that experience to Philip and his own laddish refusal to admit his distaste for a stupid bet was infuriating!

His lean powerful face set into grim lines. He had to make amends. He had misjudged her and she had paid a high price.

A kindly older woman, who introduced herself in careful English as the housekeeper, brought Lydia a menu and talked her through it. Having made her selections, Lydia went for a soak in the sunken bath and scrubbed her tummy crimson to remove the fake tattoo. Not one of her cleverest ideas, she conceded, stifling the memory of Cristiano pressing his mouth there.

Clad in a pair of short pyjamas, she checked her phone for messages. She had been hoping to hear from her mother, for she was eager for the chance to tell Virginia that she was now safe from any threat of prosecution. She reminded herself that the older woman had been so scared that it might well be a few weeks before she had the courage to make contact with her daughter. After all, Virginia had anxiously mentioned the fact that mobile phone records could be checked.

Dinner was served at a beautifully set table in the opulent reception room that linked with hers. But she ate sitting cross-legged on the bed next door, and endeavoured to watch a gardening programme on the plasma screen she found concealed with other technology behind electronic sliding doors. Replete with food, she crawled into bed. She did not think she had ever been so exhausted. It was both emotional and physical. Yet, even though she tried to bar Cristiano from her thoughts, she fell asleep with his vibrant darkly handsome image in her mind's eye.

She did not awaken until mid-morning, when a maid opened the curtains and brought her a cup of tea. Emerging from the bathroom enveloped in a towel, she went into the attached dressing room and was astonished to discover that virtually all the outfits she had tried on the night before now hung in colour-coordinated rows in the fitted closets.

She glanced at the functional garments she had already taken out, and then slowly tidied them away again.

If Cristiano wanted her to dress in the latest and most expensive fashion, was it really worth the aggro of saying no? She snatched in a sustaining breath and compressed her soft lips. It was time to deal with life as it was, not life as she would have liked it to be. Shielding her mother and escaping a likely prison sentence came at a cost that she had agreed to pay. Nobody had twisted her arm, nobody had forced her to sign that contract, she reminded herself doggedly. She was a mistress. She was an accessory, arm-candy, a trophy to be put on display. And, whether she liked it or not, presentation was everything when only her face and her body counted in the balance.

A little while later, Cristiano phoned to ask her to join him for lunch on the terrace. As if she had a choice, she thought fiercely, her pride still stinging at the awareness of how much she was in his power. In his country, in his house, in the very clothes he had chosen, and with an intimate ache at the heart of her to remind her, if she needed a reminder, of his passionate possession.

'Of course…'

'Did you sleep well?' he enquired huskily.

His dark sexy drawl made her tingle as much as though he had trailed his fingers down her slender spine. Soft pink burnished her cheeks. 'Very well.'

'You didn't even stir when I checked on you around midnight.'

Lydia stiffened and her chin tilted. 'Why did you feel the need to check on me?'

'You were upset. I wanted to be sure that you were all right—'

'Well, there was no need. I wasn't upset, just tired!'

'Okay...' Cristiano dragged the word out with amazing expressiveness.

'I'm not being unreasonable!' Lydia snapped defensively.

'I didn't say anything.'

'It was the way you said, "Okay",' she mumbled in the silence that he allowed to stretch until she was forced to make a response. 'It sounded long-suffering.'

'Why would I sound like that?' Cristiano chided silkily, and she almost threw the phone across the room.

He made her so angry—yet she had never before had a problem with her temper. At least not until she had loved and lost Cristiano Andreotti. Until he had yanked her back to him, handcuffed to a contract that made self-respect a desperate challenge. Nonetheless, yesterday she had acted the part of mistress to the manner born.

Worrying at the underside of her lower lip, she glanced in the mirror. The blue silk organza dress hung like the exclusive garment it was, clinging to her slender figure where it should, skimming where it should not.

She saw the view from the terrace before she saw Cristiano, and it was so spectacular that she walked straight over to the stone wall to gaze in wonder. Low-lying clouds wreathed a village on the far side of the valley with a misty haze that lent the ancient ring of stone medieval buildings on the hill a fairytale quality.

'It's so beautiful,' she murmured when she heard steps behind her.

'Not quite as beautiful as you, *bella mia*,' Cristiano remarked, for she looked dazzling, in a dress that reflected the sapphire-blue of her eyes, with her abundant hair simply styled to fall round her shoulders. After the restive night he had passed, striving to come to terms with the concept of giving up his freedom, he was finally willing to acknowledge that there would be one very obvious reward.

Lydia spun round and momentarily allowed herself to take her visual fill of his extreme impact in a formal dark suit. Even that elongated glance proved to be a mistake. As she looked her fingertips tingled with the memory of the warmth of his bronzed skin and the silky feel of his hair. Ready colour rose in her cheeks and she moved hurriedly towards the table that sat in the cool shade of towering chestnut trees.

Wine was poured and *antipasto* was served. The golden liquid was dry on her tongue. She didn't much like wine but, having recognised the world-famous label on the bottle, she persevered. The first course arrived, and she asked Cristiano how long he had owned the *palazzo*.

'It's been in the family for a while,' Cristiano revealed.

Lydia gave her wine another valiant tasting. 'How long is a while?'

'A couple of hundred years.' His tiny shrug dismissed the subject as of no import, and he signalled the hovering manservant to pass on some instruction.

'I really know next to nothing about your background. You're an only child, aren't you?' she pressed, determined to keep the dialogue on lines that she could handle.

'My parents didn't live together for long.' His intonation was cool, discouraging, his reserve patent in his response.

A fresh glass was set in front of her and another bottle uncorked with Italian ceremony.

'What's this?' she asked.

Cristiano laughed. 'You're drinking what you've got as though it's cough medicine. I requested something sweeter.'

His acute observation powers mortified her, but he

made light conversation with enviable ease and the food was fabulous. Slowly, she began to relax.

'I have something important to say to you,' he murmured gravely at the end of the meal.

Her blood ran cold. 'You've had enough of me already and you're sending me home?'

'No, I don't want to let you go,' Cristiano confessed without apology.

She felt almost light-headed at that news, and the realisation shook her. Was that *relief* she was feeling? Surely not? Bewilderment and shame threatened her composure, for she was finding it increasingly hard to comprehend her own reactions around Cristiano.

His crystal glass casually cupped in one lean brown hand, Cristiano rose and strolled across the terrace into the hot sunlight, before looking back at her. 'I reached certain conclusions last night,' he admitted flatly. 'I have treated you in a way I have treated no other woman.'

'How nice to be singled out as unique!' But although she tried to sound insouciant, she was dry-mouthed with stress at the prospect of what he might be about to say next.

His stunning eyes were pure lethal gold. 'It's not a joking matter. I will be frank…from the hour you took off with Stevens, I thought of you as a total slapper.'

That was frank indeed, and she reddened.

'And I was wrong. You're the exact opposite. You, on the other hand, thought I was real bastard, and you were right to think that,' he spelt out with sardonic cool. 'The business with the bet was indefensible, and the contract was designed to entrap and demean.'

She gripped her fine porcelain coffee cup so hard she was surprised that the handle didn't break off. She stared at the immaculate white linen tablecloth, her heart beating very fast.

'I owe you...I owe you big-time.' Cristiano breathed hard and low, as if the very words were being forced from him.

Lydia glanced up in surprise.

His lean strong face was sombre. 'I do have honour. I do have standards. I can't change the past, though. It seems that you've won this round hands down...I'm willing to marry you.'

CHAPTER SEVEN

LYDIA stared at Cristiano, unable to credit what he had said and scarcely daring to breathe in the hot still air. 'M-marry me?' she stammered shakily. 'You're *willing* to marry me?'

Cristiano tossed back the contents of his wine glass with seemingly little appreciation for the vintage. 'There will be some consolations. I find you incredibly desirable, *gioia mia.*'

'I'm thrilled.' Lydia cast her throwaway comment while very different emotions assailed her. Hurt pride, disappointment and pain combined inside her in a volatile mix. Once a proposal of marriage from Cristiano would have been her every dream come true. But his ambivalence, his reluctance to marry her, was almost comically obvious. Dully, she wondered why she wasn't laughing.

Cristiano dealt her a brooding look of dark cynicism. 'Of course you are.'

She wanted to hit him. He knew what a rich prize he was in terms of looks, status and wealth. It did not seem to occur to him that a woman might expect something more than those superficial attributes from him. Or that he might meet with a refusal.

'How do you feel about me?'

Cristiano shot her a frowning appraisal, his stubborn jawline clenching. 'What's that supposed to mean?'

Lydia was as pale as death, her fingers knotted below the level of the table and then frantically crossing for luck. 'You're not stupid. You know.'

'I don't do love—just sex,' he asserted very drily.

'I'm not cheap. I'll only marry for love!' She managed to force a laugh that was convincing enough at least not to shatter the glass in her vicinity, but deep down inside she felt as if a steamroller had gone over her vital organs. The crazy wheeling and dipping of her thoughts bewildered her as much as the distinct downward plunge of her spirits.

Cristiano rested unamused night-dark eyes on her. 'I appreciate that I've taken you very much by surprise.'

A tremor ran through her taut length. She was in a state of shock, and almost pointed out that an announcement of his nuptial plans would make headlines round the world. 'Yes, you have—'

'But I don't like your attitude,' he said bluntly.

Every scrap of colour ebbed from her lovely face and she bent her head, fighting for the control not to snap back at him. Her first marriage proposal and it was an insult. He knew his own worth too well. He saw no reason why he should dress up the degrading reality that all he wanted was her body on tap. He regarded her as a lesser being, whom he would be honouring with his name and his riches. Her role was to be a grateful recipient, scarcely able to believe her good fortune. Unfortunately torture could not have dragged such a humble response from her at that moment. How dared he think that she would take him on such terms? How dared he tell her to her face that sex was all she had to offer him? She hated him. That was all she was sure of just then. Hatred and pain were like a twisting knife inside her and she couldn't think beyond that.

'I'm sorry you don't like my attitude,' she said woodenly, staring a hole in the tablecloth. 'But I wouldn't want to marry someone like you.'

The tension was appalling. She was so stiff she was afraid a sudden movement would shatter her into tiny pieces, and the silence seethed around her like a menacing storm. She had offended him, and his displeasure chilled the atmosphere.

'Look at me…'

And she looked, even though she didn't want to look, for the habit of command was so engrained in him that she could not resist its powerful pull. He surveyed her with impassive dark eyes and she shivered.

'You're saying no?'

Like a marionette on strings, she nodded, hardly daring to credit her own nerve. Yet the more his formidable assurance and presence intimidated her, the harder she fought to remain untouched and unaffected.

Pure outrage leapt in Cristiano. He could not believe it. Unless there was someone else she cared about. But how likely was that when she had been a virgin? A celibate, very moral someone else? Some dead guy? He suppressed that unusually imaginative train of thought with icy distaste. Could she dislike him so much? He rammed that reflection back down into his subconscious while mercilessly crushing that disturbing sense of outrage stonedead. He had made the offer. If she was too foolish to appreciate the advantages of becoming his wife, honour at least had been satisfied. She had done him a favour. For the first time he reminded himself that she was a thief, and just as quickly he was marvelling that he had ever contrived to overlook that reality and even considered marrying her.

While Lydia watched, Cristiano checked the time and murmured without expression, 'We're flying to London early tomorrow morning.'

Her spine was so rigid it ached. 'Are we? But we only got here yesterday.'

'This is how my life is. I have a board meeting at the UK office.'

'Right,' Lydia muttered, her entire focus locked to him in bemusement. Was that it? Was that really it? Was there to be no further discussion of that staggering proposal? It seemed not. The savage tension had already vanished as though it had never been. He appeared cool, indifferent.

'And you have an appointment to keep with the Happy Holidays charity.'

Her eyes opened very wide, and even though she assumed she had misheard him, she lost colour. 'I beg your pardon…?'

'I'm afraid that, regardless of how you feel, you will have to bite the bullet and smile throughout the proceedings.'

'What proceedings?'

'My staff have organised a photo opportunity and reception to which the press have been invited. You will officially hand over a cheque for the money you were accused of stealing,' Cristiano explained with unnerving calm.

Her stomach executed a nervous somersault. 'You're joking!'

'No. I have never regarded theft as a laughing matter. You do not have a choice on this one.'

Even though she had not been responsible for stealing the money in the first place, Lydia still cringed at the threat of being forced to meet the charity personnel again. 'I won't do it!'

'You *will* do it. The charity has agreed. It's a PR exercise. You're part of my life now, and your reputation must be rehabilitated,' Cristiano advanced without apology.

'But everybody's going to know it's your money I'm handing over!' she protested, rising from her seat in her distress. 'What's the point?'

'People may well wonder if it's my money, but they will no longer feel so certain of your guilt. Doubts will be aired. And if, in a couple of months, you are seen to perform another act of goodwill for the same charity, you will look even more like an innocent. Most will assume that the recent…unpleasantness…' he selected that word with acerbic bite '…was a storm in a teacup.'

'I won't do it,' she mumbled again, but it was like talking to a brick wall. 'I mean it, Cristiano.'

'Think of it as your penance.'

'I thought *you* were that!' she returned bitterly.

'Would you really prefer to carry the label of thief for the rest of your life?'

That derisive question cut through her defences and she swallowed hard. Years from now, who knew what her life might be? Her supposed theft might well come back to haunt her when she least expected it. His argument was unanswerable. She supposed it was best if the whole shameful episode could be decently buried with a show for the sake of appearances. But the very thought of having to face the Happy Holidays fundraising team again filled Lydia with dread.

'I thought not,' Cristiano murmured drily.

'I can't believe you asked me to marry you…' Lydia heard herself say with an abruptness that startled her. She flushed to the roots of her hair. She had truly not meant to voice that tactless reminder, but the thought had raced straight into reckless speech.

Cristiano was more than equal to that sudden diplomatic challenge. Angling brilliant dark golden eyes over her, he drawled with unblemished cool, 'Fact is often stranger than fiction.'

A manservant came to a tactful halt at the other end of the terrace and Cristiano spoke to him. 'Your Italian teacher has arrived for your first lesson,' he told her.

Her face was perplexed. 'You never did explain why you want me to learn Italian.'

He raised a sardonic brow. 'You will be a more useful hostess with it than without.'

A cheerful little man in his early sixties greeted them both in excellent English. After chatting for a few minutes, Cristiano left them. The teacher informed her that he would be concentrating on her ability to use conversational Italian. She listened with a fixed smile but she was a thousand miles away, thinking about Cristiano and wondering if she would ever understand him.

Why had he offered marriage when he so clearly didn't want to marry her? But perhaps being a wife would have been preferable to being a mistress…? That thought crept up on her and lingered even when she tried to shut it out. Well, it was too late for a change of heart now, wasn't it? In any case, she didn't want to be married to a guy who felt nothing for her, and she wouldn't marry him for the lifestyle he could give her. At least she was hanging on to a modicum of self-respect that way.

She dined alone that evening, and wandered through the

beautiful gardens, which were kept in immaculate order. She did not see Cristiano before she finally went up to bed, and although she lay tense as a bowstring while she waited, wondering if he would come to her, she was left undisturbed.

She couldn't sleep. She tossed and turned, wrestling with her seesawing emotions, until she finally shamefacedly acknowledged disappointment.

Cristiano went through a couple of reports with his staff on the flight to London, while Lydia slumbered, curled up in an unselfconscious heap like a child. He covered her with a blanket.

While he worked, every so often he would raise his head and his keen gaze would rest with cool probing force on her delicate sleep-flushed profile. It was rare for anyone to surprise him, but she managed that feat on a regular basis. She fought with him. She melted into his arms and then told him she hated him. He had a Byzantine mind of surpassing shrewdness. He liked things to add up, and her behaviour didn't. If there was another guy, dead or alive, he wanted to know about him. This was a live-in relationship, the most serious thing he had ever got into with a woman. It would probably only last a couple of months, but it would only be sensible to find out everything there was to know about her. He would have her checked out by a private detective agency.

'What time is this photo opportunity with the Happy Holidays crew kicking off?' Lydia asked tautly in the limo that was ferrying them through the London traffic.

'Two this afternoon.' He skimmed a glance over her pale tight profile. 'I don't know what you're worried about. Nobody in the charity team will dare to be unkind. My patronage is worth too much to them. As for the press, you'll just have to keep your smile pinned on and take what you get thrown at you.'

Having proffered that dollop of cold comfort in a bracing tone, Cristiano told her that he would see her later. The limo nosed in by the kerb, his bodyguards leapt out, and he vacated the limo and strode into the Andreotti building. She breathed in slow and deep. She promised herself that she would get through the day by dealing with it in small manageable bites.

Only then did it occur to her that her mother might well see a newspaper photo of her daughter handing over a cheque to the charity. Her eyes brightened. That would certainly signal the all-clear for her parent to get back in touch again. That cheering prospect made the coming ordeal seem well worthwhile.

Having pushed through his own agenda as usual, and been listened to in hushed silence by his awe-inspired board members, Cristiano emerged from the meeting in good form. His most senior PA approached him, wearing a curious air of anxiety.

'Problems?' Cristiano enquired with a raised brow.

'A Gwenna Powell has requested a meeting with you, and she's a very insistent woman.'

Cristiano frowned. 'Gwenna...*Powell*?'

The PA cleared his throat. 'I understand that she's related to Lydia Powell.'

Intrigued, Cristiano gave instructions for the lady to be shown into his office. Minutes later, a small brunette wearing a belligerent expression arrived.

'I'm Lydia's cousin,' she announced.

Cristiano was amused. He strolled forward, introduced

himself with unassailable cool, and suggested she sit down. 'What can I do for you?'

Gwenna Powell ignored the seat set out for her and dug into her capacious satchel bag instead. From it she withdrew a document which she tossed down on his desk like a challenge. Cristiano did not need to lift it to identify it as a copy of the contract that both he and Lydia had signed.

'Lydia asked me to check her post and open anything that seemed important. Imagine my horror when I discovered that she had been asked to sign *that* horrendous legal agreement!'

'My relationship with Lydia is of a private nature.' Cristiano was noting that, though there might be no physical likeness between the cousins, Lydia was also impulsive, spirited and quick-tempered. The melodic lilt of the brunette's accent was equally familiar.

In censorious unimpressed silence, Gwenna Powell removed a photoframe from her bag and extended it to him.

His ebony brows drawing together, Cristiano accepted the item. He studied the faded snapshot in considerable surprise. 'But this is an old photo of me...taken from a newspaper?'

'Yes, Mr Andreotti. You were Lydia's idol long before she ever met you. She was a schoolgirl of fourteen years of age when she framed that and you became her pin-up...'

'*Pin-up...*' Cristiano repeated huskily, surveying his own image while he absorbed this new and fabulously fascinating fact. He was attempting to imagine Lydia at that tender age, snipping his photograph out of a newspaper. She had been modelling by then, he recalled with a frown. She would have been very tall and skinny, and very beautiful, but still indisputably a child in his eyes. A whole new dimension had just been added to his knowledge of her. It was like being handed the key to a secret drawer that he couldn't wait to open.

'I want you to feel thoroughly ashamed of yourself,' Gwenna informed him. 'Lydia deserves a decent man, who respects her.'

'I asked her to marry me and she wouldn't have me,' Cristiano admitted, taking the wind from his visitor's sails in a spectacular feat of one-upmanship. 'Perhaps I failed to live up to that teenage fantasy.'

Gwenna Powell goggled at him.

Cristiano set the photo with the contract and carefully stowed both items away. His, 'May I keep this?' was purely rhetorical. He offered tea and was equally politely refused. His diminutive visitor appeared to have taken fright at his mention of a proposal, and was eager to take her leave.

'Will you tell Lydia that I came to see you?' she asked worriedly before she departed.

'No,' Cristiano asserted, without a second of hesitation.

When his PA came in with some figures that had been requested, he found Cristiano in a curiously abstracted mood. Thirty minutes later, his employer made several rapid phone calls and announced that he was finishing early.

Impervious to the effect of such a declaration voiced by a male who routinely put in eighteen-hour days, Cristiano left the office.

A rather domineering young woman from a PR firm accompanied Lydia to the exclusive hotel chosen for the event. Her nerves were like jumping beans. Back at the apartment, she had agonised about what to wear before finally choosing a black and grey fitted jacket and pencil skirt that Cristiano had picked to meet the requirements of the 'stuffy' sections of his social life.

When she entered the function room, her companion took her straight over to the charitable team, and a rather uncomfortable conversation ensued in which everyone talked too much and smiled too often. The three models whom Lydia had persuaded to volunteer for the fashion show four months earlier arrived together. As all but one had made angry phone calls to her when the story of the cheques that had bounced first hit the newspapers, Lydia had once again to rise above her embarrassment.

'I'm relieved that you got the mess sorted out,' one of the girls remarked with a reproving sniff.

'Yes, being associated with all those nasty rumours flying around didn't do much for my image.'

'I know. I'm really glad you could all be here today, and I'm sorry about all the fuss there's been,' Lydia said with genuine gratitude.

The third model was a staggeringly lovely Russian redhead called Helenka. Her sinuous curves and languorous appeal were showcased in a revealing short white dress. A rising superstar, with a firm sense of her superiority, Helenka flashed Lydia a scornful look. 'We've agreed that we don't want to feature in any photos with you.'

Lydia reddened as if she had been slapped. The PR woman at her elbow waded in to protest that that was unworkable, and moved away several feet to employ her mobile phone. Members of the press were already arriving. Lydia was uneasily aware that any sign of a rift between her and the other models would swiftly be seized on to make a better story.

In the midst of the discussion, Helenka vented an exclamation and pushed rudely past Lydia. 'I see a friend…'

As a whisper of comment ran round the room like an electric current, Lydia began to turn her head.

'It's Cristiano Andreotti… Oh, my word. Is he gorgeous? Or is he gorgeous?' one of the models gasped ecstatically.

A sense of relief surging through her tense body, Lydia spun round. He could only have come to support her. The tingle of awareness that his presence always caused danced through her nerve-endings like a wake-up call.

'All that, and oodles and oodles of cash into the bargain…this close to a billionaire I feel faint!' her friend proclaimed.

In the act of moving in Cristiano's direction, Lydia froze. Helenka already had a confident hand on Cristiano's arm and she was chattering to him with pointed familiarity. He glanced over at Lydia so briefly that she wasn't quite sure it had really happened, and then he laughed at something the redhead said.

Lydia was directed to the front to pose with the dummy cheque while the Happy Holidays director said a few words.

All Lydia was conscious of was that Cristiano was smiling down at Helenka and having wine brought to her. Lydia's tummy churned, a lump forming in her tight throat. She knew the buzz of grabbing Cristiano's full attention, and the Russian girl was flirting like mad with him. Lydia hovered, waiting for him to acknowledge her, but it didn't happen. Press interest was now firmly focused on the couple. A few minutes later, Helenka strolled like a queen over to a gilded chaise longue and reclined there. Lydia and the other models were urged to join her for a group photo. There were no objections to Lydia's inclusion because Helenka was much too busy directing sultry smiles at Cristiano. Afterwards, Helenka surged back to Cristiano's side, and delighted in the cameras taking note of the fact.

Arnaldo approached Lydia. 'Miss Powell? The car's ready when you are.'

Lydia blinked. 'Did your boss tell you to take me home?'

For all his size, Arnaldo looked as if he very much wanted to run when faced with that awkward question.

'Never mind…' Mustering as much dignity as she could, Lydia would not let herself glance back in Cristiano's direction.

They left the hotel by a discreet side entrance. Her legs were all wobbly. She felt sick, frightened, shocked beyond belief. Cristiano had ignored her as though she didn't exist. She would not have believed it had it not happened before her own eyes. He had acted as if she was of no more account to him than a stranger.

But evidently Helenka amused him, and he had chosen to be with the sultry Russian and send Lydia away. Was she supposed to accept that rejection with grace and in-difference? Why did she feel so absolutely gutted that she couldn't think straight? Shouldn't she be rejoicing at the possibility that Cristiano might already be planning to replace her with a more exciting lover? After all, she would then get her freedom back. She would be able to return to her own life. But could a guy who had only asked her to marry him a day earlier cool off that fast?

There had been nothing emotional about Cristiano's proposal. He had, however, found her response offensive. No doubt he had swiftly regretted the sense of honour and conscience that had prompted that proposal in the first place. Certainly, he had been very cold with her afterwards. He had kept his distance the previous night as well. Helenka was stunning, and much more sophisticated. Lydia's eyes misted over with tears. What was the matter with her? The tears rolled down her cheeks. She felt…she *felt*… Gritting her teeth, she wiped her face with the back of her hand. It was only when she was fumbling through her bag in search of a tissue that she finally noticed that there was a package on the seat beside her.

The gift tag carried her name. She lifted the parcel and tore the paper off to expose a jewel case. It bore the gold logo of an internationally renowned jeweller. An incredibly sparkly diamond bracelet nestled in a cushion of blue silk. Her mouth wobbled. She was being dumped, and she should be pleased. This was her freedom: the right to her own bed and diamonds into the bargain!

The car door opened and she climbed out. Disorientated by the discovery that the driver had ferried her to an airfield, she stared at the second limo that was disgorging Cristiano only ten yards away. In bewilderment she froze to the spot and stared. He was so breathtakingly handsome that it almost hurt her to look at him.

'You can keep that stupid bracelet!' she screeched at him, without even knowing that she was going to say that.

Cristiano studied her in polite astonishment. 'What's the matter with you?'

'I saw you with Helenka—'

'Talking.'

'You were smiling, flirting—'

'And you were jealous,' Cristiano slotted in, smooth as glass.

Her mouth opened and shut again. Fuming with rage at that accusation, she snatched in a ragged breath and blasted back at him, full volume. 'I've never heard anything so ridiculous…I was *not* jealous!'

A wicked smile that was pure provocation curved Cristiano's wide sensual mouth. The silence simmered. He said nothing.

'I was *not* jealous!' Lydia launched back at him again. 'You're famous for being a womanising rat, but I won't put up with that kind of behaviour! I'm delighted that we're breaking up!'

'But we're not breaking up, *gioia mia*. We're flying down to Southampton to board *Lestara*.'

With no grasp whatsoever of what he was talking about, Lydia could not hide her confusion. 'But I thought the bracelet in the car was a goodbye present…'

'I'm not that tacky. When it's over, I'll tell you.'

She raised an uncertain hand to her pounding brow. 'But you didn't speak to me at the hotel. You let me leave the reception alone—'

'The press can find out we're together at some other occasion. I like my privacy. I didn't want our relationship to overshadow the whole purpose of the photo session, which was to re-establish your reputation,' Cristiano murmured, walking gracefully closer to her rigid figure. 'The PR firm called to warn me that Helenka was playing up, so I set out to distract her—'

Her lips felt clumsy as she parted them. 'You distracted her…'

'It averted the attention of the press from you as well. The journalists were more interested in the idea that I might have something going with Helenka than in asking you about your time in police custody,' Cristiano pointed out. 'It also worked a treat with Helenka, who chose not to act the diva in my presence and submitted to the photos.'

Those ramifications were too much for Lydia to take in just then. The source of her deepest misgivings was still his manner towards the beautiful Russian model. 'It was obvious that you already *knew* Helenka very well!'

'She did a series of television ads for a company of mine last year. Didn't you know that?'

She shook her head. She was out of touch with the modelling world and rarely watched television. She could not bring herself to ask if the acquaintance had been an intimate one. She swallowed with difficulty and said tightly, 'She wants you…'

'But I want you, *cara mia.*'

That husky assurance set up a chain reaction through Lydia's unbearably tense body. She was shaking, and her knees were threatening to fold beneath her. She wanted to cry. Even though that horrendous sense of humiliation had evaporated, she still wanted to cry. A storm of emotion had sent her out of control, and now she was struggling to accept that it had only been a simple misunderstanding.

He had not betrayed her or rejected her. He had not preferred Helenka. Their affair, so recently begun, was not yet over. Regardless, she had made a horrible jealous scene—and a total fool of herself. How could she be jealous of him? How could she possibly be possessive of a guy she professed to hate? But she *had* been jealous, bitterly jealous, when she'd seen him laughing and smiling with Helenka. It took great courage for her to make that inner admission, and in doing so she was confronted by a much worse fear. Had she been weak enough to fall in love with him again?

Cristiano curved steadying hands to her waist and gazed down at her strained face. He wondered why that stupid scene had not made him angry, for he had little tolerance for such displays in public places. His security team had retreated behind the limos in an effort to hide their amusement. But he could see that she was not aware of their surroundings or their audience. She was still very worked up. He looked down at her, and suddenly he wanted her so badly that if there had been a hotel within reach he would have rushed her there. Disconcerted by an urge that lacked his trademark self-discipline, he tensed.

A sob was locked in Lydia's throat. She met his smouldering dark golden eyes and it was like shock therapy, for all thought of tears vanished as though it had never been. That devouring appraisal sent a frisson of helpless excitement rippling through her slight taut frame.

'Our luggage should be on the helicopter by now. We should board,' Cristiano murmured thickly, and even though he knew he should not he cupped the soft swell of her hips to bring her into closer contact with his long powerful thighs. It was an act of pure sexual provocation.

A tiny little whimper of sound, only loud enough to be heard by him, was wrested from her as she felt the hard hungry swell of his arousal against her tummy. She tilted forward into his big powerful frame, suddenly boneless with need. With a ragged laugh, he turned her round with sure confident hands and headed her in the direction of the waiting helicopter.

CHAPTER EIGHT

LYDIA was in a daze. Mercifully the racket of the helicopter rotors made speech impossible during the flight, and she sat back in her comfortable seat to recoup her energies.

She had no idea where Cristiano was taking her, and she didn't much care either. Although she thought he had mentioned Southampton she wasn't sure, and she believed she must have been mistaken—for, on reflection, it did not strike her as an exotic enough destination for Cristiano. Whatever, she had lived on her nerves all day, and felt that she had more important things to worry about.

First and foremost, she refused to credit that she could be developing any form of emotional attachment to Cristiano Andreotti. Sex was the only hold he had on her, she told herself vehemently. It was shameful and disgusting, and it made her hate herself, but at least it wasn't love. Only an absolute dimwit would fall for a man in such circumstances, and she was not one. Nor had she any plans to become one.

Cristiano set the jewel case she had abandoned in the limo on her lap.

Lydia passed it back like a hot potato that might burn her fingers.

Out of the corner of her eye, she watched him flip up the lid and remove the bracelet. It lay across his lean brown fingers like a white river of glittering fire. He caught her hand in his and attached the bracelet to her wrist. Angrily she turned her head. He was only inches from her, brilliant golden eyes challenging. Her breath caught in her throat. He meshed his fingers into the silvery fair fall of her hair and took her soft pink mouth in a savagely intoxicating kiss that made the blood drum through her veins at an insane rate.

'Why are you so stubborn?' he demanded in stark reproof.

Lips tingling from that deeply sensual assault, Lydia turned away to gaze into space and sink deeper into her thoughts. If she didn't fight his power over her at every opportunity, where would she be? His charismatic strength and assurance were traits that she found dangerously attractive and exciting. But that did not mean that total surrender was an option for her. On her wrist the bracelet glinted and gleamed like a mocking reminder of her exact boundaries.

As the helicopter settled down on a landing pad, Lydia surfaced from her reverie and unclipped her seat belt. She caught a glimpse of the view through the front windscreen and saw some sort of a giant pulley, and beyond that rails and industrial buildings that looked like warehouses. Maybe Cristiano was coming here on business, she reflected, submitting to the necessity of letting him lift her out of the craft because he was too impatient to wait for steps. A vaguely familiar smell made her nostrils flare and she stiffened when she identified it. It was the salty fresh scent of the seaside, and her tummy immediately knotted into a little cramp of alarm.

Cristiano was guiding her towards an open door. But she was hesitating, seeking to identify her surroundings. Horror was nudging at the back of her mind and she was striving rigorously to control it. She was walking on a metal-surfaced floor, and several feet away were the polished railings that reminded her very much of a documentary about the wreck of the *Titanic*. She sucked in a rasping breath, yanked her hand free of his and moved towards the railings.

'Lydia…?' Cristiano turned back, wondering why she was being so quiet.

'This is…this is a ship,' she breathed, in what he took to be a tone of excitement.

'A boat—my yacht *Lestara*.' For the very first time Cristiano was proud of his floating palace. They would cruise in total peace and privacy. He would choose some places that she would enjoy seeing, and the yacht would dock there for them to go ashore. There would be no set itinerary. The paparazzi would never be able to track them. She would love that freedom. She would relax and unwind and stop talking nonsense about hating him. His veiled gaze gleamed with satisfaction.

Lydia forced herself inch by inch closer and peered sickly through the terrifying gaps in the rails. It was a long, long way down, but there it was, the substance of her worst nightmares: water in perpetual motion, and beneath its surface the terrifying churning dark depths that had claimed the lives of her father and her brother. Her skin was turning clammy, perspiration breaking out on her brow.

'I don't like boats,' she whispered chokily.

Cristiano laughed. 'It's a very big boat, Lydia.'

'I feel sick…'

'You couldn't possibly be feeling seasick,' he told her wryly. 'We haven't even sailed yet.'

While Cristiano watched in frank disbelief, Lydia threw up over the side of the yacht. He went immediately to her assistance, pressing an immaculate handkerchief on her and urging her away from the railings. 'Let's get you inside…'

But Lydia didn't want to go inside. All she wanted was to be off the boat and back on to dry land again. She was attempting to withstand a hysterical desire to throw herself back into his helicopter.

'I don't like the sea,' she confided tautly.

'Then don't look at it,' Cristiano countered, as if he was dealing with a fractious child. 'You must have eaten something that disagreed with you. I'll ask the doctor to check you over.'

'I don't need a doctor.' When he wasn't looking at her, Lydia crammed a fist against her wobbling mouth, tears standing out in her eyes.

Cristiano took her straight to a huge and opulent state room, but she was only interested in the washing facilities. From a window she saw the sea, seemingly so tranquil, with the summer sunlight shining on the water, and she was sick again.

'Go away,' she told him wretchedly, her teeth chattering together with misery.

Ignoring her feeble remonstrations, Cristiano carried her out of the superb marble bathroom across to the wide bed, where he rested her down and pressed a cool cloth to her pounding brow. 'The doctor will arrive at any moment, *cara mia.*'

'Don't you understand? I'll be fine if you take me off this boat!'

'When did you last eat? You slept through breakfast on the flight from Italy. Did you have any lunch?'

'I'm just sick with fear!' she gasped strickenly.

'But there's nothing to be afraid of…'

Suddenly it was all too much, and she burst into floods of tears, sobs racking her slight body where she lay on the bed. He cradled her in his arms and pulled her against him, urging her to calm down. He didn't understand, and she knew he didn't. Running away, surrendering to fear, was anathema to him. He could not comprehend her irrational terror. She fought that suffocating darkness in her mind long enough to say, 'My father and my brother drowned…'

Cristiano was suddenly still. He looked down at her pale tormented face and read the truth of those desperate words in her haunted eyes. *I don't like boats…I don't like the sea.* He wrapped his arms tightly round her.

'I'm sorry…I'm very sorry,' he intoned half under his breath. 'We'll leave as soon as the doctor has seen you.'

A knock on the door announced the doctor's arrival. The two men spoke in low voices and Cristiano returned to her side. 'Will you accept an injection to ease the sickness?'

'And then we'll leave…immediately?' she pressed frantically.

'I promise.' He gripped her hand.

She was so overwrought that she was supersensitive to everything, and she flinched from the tiny prick of the injection in her arm. A miasma of drowsiness crept over her. Her sense of time ebbed. Her frantic thoughts were dulled, her limbs increasingly heavy. She pressed her cheek into Cristiano's jacket, the achingly familiar scent of him washing over her like a soothing balm, and fell asleep.

* * *

Lydia dreamt that she was trapped deep under water. Her lungs burning, she struggled frantically to break free and find her little brother. She was calling his name and only bubbles were coming out.

'Lydia…'

Her terrified eyes flew wide on a softly lit room. She was sobbing for breath, hopelessly disorientated, her skin damp.

'That was some bad dream.' Cristiano was hunkered down by the side of the bed so that their eyes were level. 'I could hear you yelling from next door.'

'It's always the same dream,' she whispered shakily. 'I hate it!'

'You need something to eat.' Vaulting upright, he picked up the phone by the bed.

She pulled herself up against the pillows. Registering that she was naked, she anchored the sheet below her arms. Her eyes had adjusted to the dim light and she knew where she was: back in the master bedroom of the penthouse apartment in London. She reached for his hand and turned his wrist to check the time on his watch. 'For goodness' sake,' she exclaimed, when she realised it was one in the morning.

'That injection really knocked you out, but you needed the rest,' Cristiano contended.

'I don't remember flying back—'

'We travelled by limo. With you fast asleep, it made more sense.' He was wearing cream chinos that sat low on his lean hips, and a black shirt. Even though it was the middle of the night, and he was badly in need of a shave, he still looked drop-dead gorgeous.

'I'm sorry…you must've thought I'd gone off my head or something,' she muttered in a mortified rush. 'But I haven't been on a boat since…well, since the accident. I suppose that's pretty gutless of me, but until today I was always able to avoid it.'

'You were with your father and brother when they died?' Cristiano queried in surprise. 'What age were you?'

'Ten. Robert was only six,' she framed unevenly. 'We were on holiday in Mallorca. Dad used to take us down to the beach to watch the motor boats racing about. I asked him to take us out on one, and we went on the last day. He took us round the headland because the bay was so busy. He said it would be safer, but it meant we couldn't be seen from the beach. And before you ask, no, we weren't wearing lifejackets…'

'What happened, *cara mia*?' Cristiano used the question to break the heavy silence that had fallen.

'A couple of other boats passed us, and then this big wave came over the edge of the boat and water came in. It happened so fast I couldn't believe it. Robert was screaming, Dad was panicking, and the boat capsized. Apparently Dad hit his head on something and was knocked out. All I know is that I n-never saw him alive again.'

Cristiano closed both hands round the fingers she had tightly knotted together. 'You…? Your little brother…?'

'I was thrown clear…but he was caught under the boat. I was a good swimmer…I went underwater but I couldn't find him. It was so dark, and there was a strong current. A fishing boat came, and they got Robert out, but it was too late.'

'It's a miracle you survived.'

A sob was wrested from her and she pulled her fingers free of his to cover her face, for the recollection of that tragic day still haunted her. 'It was my fault… If I hadn't begged, we'd never have been in that boat.'

'That's nonsense. You were a child. It was an accident.

Nobody should be allowed to go sailing without life preservers. What was your nightmare about?'

And she told him. It had been a very long time since she had talked about that day, or its repercussions, and he was a surprisingly good listener. So she told him about how her mother had gone to pieces after the boating accident, and how her father's business had gone belly-up within months.

When it had all been aired, she felt a surprising sense of relief, and the past settled back into the recesses of her memory. Only then did she put a hand up to brush her hair from her brow and register that, after hours of sleep, it was a tangle of tousled waves and she probably looked a real mess.

'I could do with a shower.' Forgetting that she was naked as the day she was born, she pushed back the sheet and scrambled out of bed. With a moan of embarrassment, she raced for the bathroom to the sound of his laughter.

'You have five minutes before we eat,' he warned her cheerfully.

Wrapped in a big towel, her wet hair slicked back from her brow, she emerged again, thoroughly scrubbed, squeaky clean and breathless. He was lounging back on the bed, watching the business news.

A trolley of food awaited them in the room next door.

Hurriedly tucking in the end of her towel as it pulled free, Lydia muttered, 'I should get dressed.'

'I forbid it, *bella mia.*' Pulling out a chair for her occupation, Cristiano dealt her a slow-burning smile of sensual appreciation. 'Why put on clothes that I'm only going to take off again?'

She blushed, while a tiny wicked twist of anticipation leapt low in her pelvis. Once again her own sensuality took her by surprise and filled her with chagrin. He only had to look at her in a certain way and she was gripped by a fever of wanton longing. He knew it too. That awareness made her cringe, and she focused her attention on her meal and ate with appetite.

'Aren't you having anything?'

'I dined earlier.' He cradled a glass of red wine in one lean hand. 'I'm relieved to see that you can eat a healthy meal…you skip too many.'

'The last few months have been stressful. But let's not talk about that,' she said hastily, for she was reluctant to drag up anything controversial that might spoil the relaxed mood between them. 'Now you know all about me, isn't it time for you to talk about *you*?'

'Me…?' Taken aback, Cristiano frowned.

'Your mum…your dad—just that sort of basic stuff.' Lydia pushed her empty plate away. 'Who were they? Are they still alive?

Cristiano groaned and sprang upright. 'They're both dead. That's all a matter of public record.'

'Well, I don't know it…please,' she pressed, rising from her seat as well.

Cristiano closed a hand over hers and walked her back into the bedroom with a distinct air of masculine purpose. 'Do you want me to start, "Once upon a time"?'

'Was your childhood like a fairytale?'

Cristiano settled her down against the pillows and stepped back as though to admire the picture she made. 'Not at all—although the *palazzo* is the family castle and money was always plentiful. My mother was an heiress, very rich and very spoilt.'

Lydia was hungry for detail. 'Did she look like you? Was she beautiful?'

'I believe she was considered so.' His lean dark face had

a bleak light as he undid his shirt and stretched out beside her. Even though she tried to resist the urge, his long, lithe powerful physique drew her gaze. 'She wasn't the maternal type. I was an accident, and my nannies knew me better than she ever did. She liked to be amused, and I wasn't an amusing kid.'

'What about your father?'

'An entrepreneur of great brilliance and very success-ful—but he was my mother's slave.' Cristiano could not hide his distaste. 'She had endless affairs. She dragged his name in the dirt, slept around, and laughed in his face. He couldn't live with her and he couldn't live without her. When I was eighteen he found her in bed with one of my friends, and that night he shot himself...she didn't even attend the funeral.'

Lydia flinched, appalled by that flat recitation of the distressing facts and the horrendous scandal that must have marred his youth. She leant over him, sapphire-blue eyes bright with sympathy. 'I don't know what to say...'

He wound two fingers slowly, enticingly, into her hair, and used the silky waves to draw her down to him. Hot dark golden eyes entrapped hers. 'Then show me, *gioia mia.*'

Her eyes drifted shut when he kissed her, her heart thudding very hard against her breastbone, anticipation running like a fiery river of molten lava through her. 'Cristiano...' she whispered, feeling the sensitive peaks of her breasts tighten and throb below the rough towelling.

He pulled back from her again, and reached up with a leisurely hand to tug loose the towel. He made a ragged sound of appreciation low in his throat when he had bared the pouting swells of her breasts. 'I love your body...I love what it does for mine.'

To steady herself, her fingers spread like a starfish on his hard muscular thigh. He stroked a tender candy-pink nipple with skilful fingers that knew a woman's body as well as his own. He listened to her breath catch, watched her tremble. His scrutiny was so intense that she muttered anxiously, 'What?'

'You want me so much and you can't hide it. I like that,' he confided thickly. 'You excite me.'

She was mesmerised by his compelling gaze. 'Do I?'

'Sex has never been this hot for me. If you tried to walk away from me now, I'd lock you up,' he swore.

'I'm not going anywhere.'

'Anywhere that I don't, *cara mia*,' Cristiano affixed with husky satisfaction, tumbling her down to him to taste her reddened mouth with an erotic intimacy that made her tummy perform a somersault.

'That's romantic…'

Cristiano tensed. 'There are more of my mother's genes in me than I like to admit. I won't be unfaithful to you, but I don't do the romantic stuff.'

'I only said that because it sounded better than admitting that the only thing I like about you is how you make me feel in bed!' Lydia snapped back at him in a defensive surge.

Cristiano laughed, tipping up her chin, pinning her under him so that he could kiss her again with slow, sensual deliberation. 'You're such a liar…such a gorgeous, sexy liar. You have so much to learn, and I will very much enjoy teaching you.'

Lydia was embarrassed and uneasy, wondering why he had so smoothly brushed off her declaration of indifference to him. 'Teaching me what?'

'How to enslave me between the sheets,' he teased,

sliding off the bed to skim away his shirt and remove his chinos. 'Methods, techniques, timing.'

'I don't want to be taught that sort of thing.' Watching him, she felt her mouth run dry. She felt as though a pool of honey was dissolving inside her, and the charge of that languorous heat made her quiver.

'Yes, you do, *gioia mia*.' Cristiano came down to her again, smoothing caressing hands over the pale skin of her narrow shoulders, leaving an invisible trail of fire where he touched her. 'Although it would take a lot of patience and discipline on my part, and right at this moment those qualities are in very short supply.'

His brilliant golden eyes were raking over her small white breasts and rosy nipples with unashamed hunger. Her face was burning, and her body was equally heated. She was breathing in short rapid spurts. Desire was in her and she couldn't suppress it. He raised her up on her knees and toyed with the tender buds until she moaned, and then he kissed her with roughened masculine need. He traced the delicate flesh between her thighs and she shivered, wanting him, needing him. It was as though her bones were melting below her super-sensitive skin. When he stroked the most tender spot of all she gasped, whimpered, momentarily losing herself within that surging tide of drowningly sweet pleasure.

'I can't bear it,' she finally cried, rising up against him, rebelling against the tormenting ache of need that drove her.

He took her without words in a storm of passion that sent response hurtling through her in a fireball of energy. Answering her wildness, he cast aside his smooth self-control and plunged into her with hard, sensual force. Frenzied excitement seized her. She had never been so attuned to him. She was stunned that he could know so exactly what she craved.

She wasn't prepared when he pulled out of her and re-arranged her almost roughly on her knees. In shock and arousal, she gasped his name.

'Trust me,' he urged raggedly.

Without hesitation he hungrily repossessed her willing body with a primal savagery that drove her out of her mind with pleasure. When her world erupted in a dazzling rush of ecstatic sensation she went with it in mindless acceptance. Convulsive waves of delight quivered through her while he vented an uninhibited growl of satisfaction and shuddered with release.

'Hmm…' Having tipped her over and drawn her back into his arms, with a hair-roughened thigh hooked over hers to hold her in place, Cristiano nuzzled her brow and sighed, 'You're sensational, *bella mia*.'

'So we can skip the lessons?' she dared, languorous with the sense of joy and contentment that always followed their passion.

Husky laughter shifted him in the circle of her arms. 'No. You can tell me why you were still a virgin when I had my wicked way with you.'

Lydia tensed, her fingers absently stroking over the satin smooth damp skin of his back. 'I was very wary, and not very interested when I was younger. Maybe I took longer to grow up than other girls. My mother had a boyfriend who tried to get into bed with me once. Nothing happened, because I screamed the place down, but he really scared me and made me feel bad about myself,' she shared. 'Mum said I must've encouraged him—'

Cristiano raised his head, his beautiful dark eyes narrowed to gleaming pinpoints of steel. 'You're kidding me? What age were you?'

'Thirteen. He'd been living with us a couple of months

when it happened.' She grimaced. 'Something about him gave me the creeps, but I could never work out what it was. Then one night, when Mum was out, he started coming on to me and I went up to bed to get away. If Mum hadn't come back early and found him in my room, I don't know what would've happened.'

'I do—and if you'd been raped I imagine your mother would've found some way to blame you for that too!' Cristiano cut in with contempt.

Lydia winced. 'Don't say that. You've got to understand how upset she was! She was hoping to marry him.'

'Her first loyalty should still have been to you.' Cristiano smoothed a surprisingly gentle forefinger down over her cheekbone and studied her. 'No wonder you were still a virgin, after that frightening introduction to the adult world of sex! I was an insensitive bastard as well. I was so hot for you I had no patience.'

'It just all feels different with you,' she muttered, unable to find the words to describe how that was when she didn't understand it herself.

'I want to hear that it feels earth-shattering with me, *gioia mia*,' he breathed in a low pitched undertone that skimmed her spine like a caress.

As she was smiling helplessly at that shameless invitation to boost an ego that required no such encouragement, Cristiano flipped back from her without warning, his lean, darkly handsome features set taut. He swore rawly in his own language.

'What's wrong?' Lydia demanded anxiously.

Cristiano stared at her with bemused golden eyes. 'I didn't use a condom. For the first time in my life, I forgot!'

Lydia tensed. 'I'm not taking anything…'

Still evidently dumbstruck by his oversight in the contraceptive stakes, Cristiano squared his aggressive jawline. 'When will we know whether or not you're pregnant?'

She reddened, and shut her eyes to recall dates and count. 'In about two weeks.'

'So right now you're at your most fertile?' he deduced. 'How do you feel about babies?'

'Never thought about them.'

'Neither have I,' Cristiano admitted, still deep in shock at his own carelessness. 'But if we're unlucky—'

'Isn't it funny how a single word can say so much? *Unlucky...*' Lydia was pale.

'All I meant to say was that I'll look after you...and the baby,' he tacked on, his accent very thick. 'So you don't need to worry about that angle.'

'I'm not worrying,' she lied, thinking how dreadful it would be to end up unintentionally pregnant by a guy whose sole source of interest in her was her ability to amuse him in bed. 'But I could go to the doctor and ask for the morning-after pill.'

'No.' Cristiano's rejection of that suggestion was immediate, and it surprised him as much as it surprised her. 'I don't want that. That wouldn't sit well with me. We'll wait and see.'

Cristiano settled back against the pillows, scrutinised her taut profile, and then eased an arm round her to pull her up against him again. 'Get some sleep and stop worrying,' he instructed huskily. 'We're heading back to Italy tomorrow.'

'I wish I qualified for air miles.'

He laughed in surprise and appreciation and doused the lights.

She snuggled in to him, imagining herself with a buggy. She really quite liked the idea, and blinked in confusion in the darkness. It would be a disaster if she *had* conceived, she reminded herself in consternation. She couldn't act like a silly kid and daydream about motherhood without considering the realities. What was happening to her? Furthermore, what had happened to that hatred she had been so certain she felt? That terrible bitterness had ebbed, although the same fear of hurt lived on inside her, she acknowledged ruefully. Was she falling for him again?

Cristiano ran a possessive hand down over a slender hip. 'How tired are you?'

'Not that tired,' she whispered breathlessly, excitement licking at her between one breath and the next, and all serious thought suspended.

A wonderful pair of stylish diamond earrings sparkled up at Lydia. She paled and, pushing the case back across the table, spun away. 'I can't accept these…I can't!'

Cristiano gave her an exasperated appraisal. 'What's the matter with you? It's a gift…you can't refuse it!'

'You've given me a necklace, a bracelet, a watch…now these. And I bet they're worth a fortune!'

'So I'm not cheap, *bella mia*. I'm generous. It's a character trait, and it's supposed to be plus in my favour.' Cristiano closed his hands over her slender wrists and tugged her inexorably closer.

Lydia resisted the temptation to point out that he needed no more pluses in his favour. She was hugely uncomfortable with the outrageous number of extravagant presents he was giving her. Did he think she expected such riches? Did he feel he had to pay for her services? Wasn't the vast sum he had paid out to the Happy Holidays charity sufficient? Whatever, her jewel box—an extremely expensive miniature antique trunk that had also been a gift—was full to overflowing with dazzling diamonds and sapphires!

'Maybe it makes me *feel* cheap,' she muttered accusingly. 'Some people would call those diamonds the wages of sin!'

Cristiano groaned in disbelief. 'You can be such a drama queen.'

'Who made me sign that horrible contract?'

Cristiano did not want to think about the contract. He locked her to him and claimed her soft pink lips with a devastating hunger that had not abated, even though they had been together without a break for weeks. 'I like structure and rules. I misjudged you. There's much more than a legal agreement operating between us now.'

Lydia wanted so badly to believe him.

The phone rang and he set her free to answer it. Strolling over to the boundary wall of the terrace, she sat down. The golden sunlight was wonderfully warm on her skin. The same glorious, timeless view of the green valley of fields and vineyards had greeted her every morning and evening for almost three weeks. She could hardly believe that she had been in Tuscany with Cristiano for so long. The days had flown, when she would have preferred every moment to pass by at a snail's pace because she was so incredibly happy.

No longer was she trying to convince herself of her undying hatred for him. She had accepted that she loved him and she wasn't ashamed of her feelings any more. When he walked into a room it was as if the sun came out inside her. When he smiled it gave her a floaty feeling. When she wakened in his arms in the morning she felt safe and contented. When he touched her, emotion and sensation came together so powerfully she had felt tears sting her eyes more than once.

It was his fault she had fallen for him, she reflected ruefully. He had been so incredibly attentive, affectionate and romantic. He might not do love, but he did do candle-lit dinners, moonlight walks through the gardens, picnics in secret glades in the forest. They had walked hand in hand through medieval hill towns, sat in sleepy restaurants talking for hours. He had taken her to see a dietician and had had to grudgingly accept that, while a few extra pounds of weight would do her no harm, she was naturally thin. He had patiently helped her with her Italian lessons. He had flown her to Paris for a concert given by her favourite singer and taken her to view the two famous gardens in the vicinity.

Was it any wonder that once or twice she had wondered if he was the same guy she had first met? After all, when they had dated he had been an incurable workaholic who would not spare the time to get to know her. But now he was continually cutting short his working hours to be with her. The change in his attitude meant a lot to her. She had decided that since she was happy, and happiness was not that easy to find, she should live for the moment and strive to forget their relationship's questionable beginnings.

Just two clouds marred her contentment. The apprehension that Cristiano's moment of forgetfulness in bed might have fertile consequences *did* worry her. She had tried not to worry too much, for she had persuaded herself that there was only a very small risk of such a development. Even so, she was firmly convinced that an unplanned pregnancy would destroy their relationship, for no male appreciated his freedom more than Cristiano.

Her greatest concern, however, related to her mother, who had still to get back in touch with her. Lydia had phoned everyone with a connection to the older woman, and had been surprised that so many of those people had told her that they hadn't seen or spoken to Virginia in months or even years. Her failure to establish a single lead to her mother's whereabouts had left Lydia feeling that she didn't know the older woman as well as she had believed. Surely her mother could not have intended to disappear from her daughter's life so completely?

'Okay…' Cristiano breathed. 'Tell me what's up.'

She sighed. 'I'm worried about my mum. I'm starting to think that she's disappeared off the face of this earth!'

'Since when?'

'Since just before I was arrested. She was afraid she'd be accused with me, and got in a panic.'

'Why? Was she involved in the fashion show as well?' Cristiano directed a look of polite enquiry at her, and she relaxed a little and advanced further details in answer to his questions. 'Would you like me to see if I can find out anything for you?'

'Yes…but I don't see how.'

'I have great resources.' Cristiano thought it likely that the results of the checks he had ordered on Lydia might well contain some useful leads. He had left that report sitting unopened and unread in London, because investigating Lydia without her knowledge had belatedly struck him as unethical. He would have it forwarded.

'I'd be really grateful. I'm worried sick about her,' Lydia admitted honestly. 'Her marriage broke up shortly before she went away, so goodness knows what sort of state of mind she might be in.'

'I'll find her for you, *cara mia*.' Cristiano consulted his watch, slanting ebony brows drawing together. 'But right now we have an appointment to keep, and we should make a move.'

Lydia gave him a puzzled glance. 'What appointment?'

Cristiano shrugged with a shade less cool than was usual. 'I think it makes sense for you to have a pregnancy test done by a doctor, so I've gone ahead and organised it.'

Lydia was truly taken aback. 'But that's crazy…I can easily buy a test.'

'A test you perform yourself might give a false result.'

Lydia flushed and lowered her lashes. Obviously he was really worried that she might have conceived. He had hidden the fact well, only casually alluding to the possibility on a couple of occasions since that night. But now it was clear that he was not prepared to wait even another couple of days to see if there was cause for a test to be done.

'If you prefer this way of going about things…that's fine,' she muttered uncomfortably.

'It's something we should share,' Cristiano decreed with assurance.

The appointment was at a private clinic. The doctor, a suave gynaecologist, left them in his smart office and reappeared with a grave expression. 'The test was negative. You're not pregnant, Miss Powell.'

Lydia was quite unprepared for the sharp stab of disappointment that afflicted her in response to that news.

Cristiano was stunned. He had firmly believed that she would be pregnant. They were both young and healthy. For fifteen years he had assiduously guarded against any possibility of conception. He had never taken a risk, made a mistake or had an accident. Was it any wonder that he had been fully convinced that one contraceptive oversight would infallibly lead to the creation of a baby? All that said, however, he reasoned, in a bewilderment that was new to him, it should still be a huge *relief* to receive the news that he was not to become a father.

Lydia was struggling to feel equally relieved. It occurred to her that in recent weeks Mother Nature had been playing games with her subconscious mind. While on the surface she had maintained a sensible attitude to the concept of an unplanned pregnancy, little daydreams, doubtless fuelled by sneaky female hormones, had made her consider the possibility of motherhood for the very first time. And the truth was that she had really warmed to the idea of having a baby.

'I'm sure you must be pleased that we don't have any-thing to worry about any more,' she muttered tautly when they were back in the limo.

Cristiano said nothing in response to that leading question. Lean, strong face impassive, he was deep in thought.

Her eyes were stinging. She was seriously embarrassed, and terrified he would notice that she was upset. A lump formed in her throat and she tried and failed to swallow. She blinked back tears furiously.

'Perhaps it is human nature to want what has been denied,' Cristiano commented. 'You're disappointed, aren't you?'

'No, I'm not!' she gasped chokily, rifling through all his pockets to find a hanky and then burying her face in it. 'It's just the tension, that's all…and now I'm feeling a little tearful.'

'I'd like to have a baby with you, *gioia mia*,' Cristiano told her, as though it was the most natural thing in the world.

CHAPTER NINE

THE hanky dropped from Lydia's nerveless fingers. Her tear-drenched blue eyes locked to his lean, darkly handsome features with dazed uncertainty, for she was unable to credit that he meant what he had said. 'Are you teasing me?'

'It's not a joking matter. I am very much in earnest,' Cristiano asserted in his dark deep drawl. 'I've realised that I would like a child.'

'Oh…' It was all she could think of to say. The thought of having a baby with Cristiano was making nonsense of all rational thought, for at that moment he was offering her what she most wanted on earth. Indeed, it shook her that her desire for a child could have gone so deep.

'I suppose it is natural.' Cristiano shifted a lean brown hand in a graceful gesture of acceptance. 'I've reached a stage in life where I'm ready to be a father. This little drama of ours has simply brought that truth home to me. I, too, was disappointed when we learned that there was not to be a child.'

'I honestly didn't know I'd feel like that,' she admitted in a rush, attempting to put her thoughts in order. 'I just can't believe that you feel the same way.'

Enquiring golden eyes rested on hers. 'Why not?'

She could've told him fifty reasons why not. Babies weren't cool lifestyle choices. Babies didn't travel well and he never stopped. But, most of all, babies deserved two parents. Although that wasn't always possible, it was definitely an objective that required serious consideration. Her thoughts were spinning like whirling dervishes, leaving her dizzy. 'I don't fancy being a single parent,' she admitted abruptly.

The silence simmered and bubbled like a witch's cauldron on the boil.

Cristiano surveyed her with inhuman calm. 'So…you have a point to make?'

Lydia went very pink and studied her linked hands. Just weeks ago he had proposed. She had shouted *no* on principle, and that had been that. She had let pride and bitterness do her talking for her. It had since occurred to her that she might have been more than a little hasty in giving him that spirited negative response. Yes, she would love to be valued for something more than her ability to entertain him in bed several times a day. On the other hand, it would be grossly unjust of her not to acknowledge that she was pleasing herself there too. Everything in the bedroom department was absolutely amazing, and she had no complaints whatsoever. In fact, on every level, life with Cristiano was wildly exceeding her expectations. He treated her so well. He made her feel incredibly happy. But she could not rely on that. He didn't love her, and inevitably their affair would run its course and come to an end.

'Lydia…?'

'Shush…I'm thinking very hard here.' She sighed, thinking worriedly that it would be very wrong to even consider having a baby in such an insecure relationship.

It didn't matter that she believed that a child would be a comfort to her when he had gone from her life. That would be a very selfish way to look at parenting, she decided shamefacedly. She had to act like a responsible adult. She might love him and want his baby but only the commitment of marriage would give them both security. How much did he want to be a father? Enough to marry her?

'Can I help?' Cristiano enquired gently.

Before she could lose her nerve, Lydia breathed in very deep, and just fired the words at him. 'I'll be happy to have a baby with you. But there's a condition.'

'No pain, no gain,' Cristiano quipped, lush black lashes low over smouldering golden eyes as he let a caressing masculine fingertip slowly skate a provocative trail down over her slender thigh, smiling when she shivered. 'But we could shelve the negotiation until sunset, and spend the afternoon working on the project, *carissima*.'

Her heart skipped a beat, and then raced with a sad lack of self-control. She shot him a sidewise glance, tummy flipping when she met his stunning eyes. 'I'm trying to have a serious talk here… What I want to say is that I'll have a baby if you marry me…'

Cristiano elevated a sleek ebony brow in apparent surprise. 'So what happened to love?'

Lydia blinked. 'I beg your pardon?'

'You said you would only marry for love,' he reminded her smoothly.

Lydia blushed to the roots of her hair and shifted uneasily on her seat. 'Well, perhaps that was a bit…er…fanciful,' she selected in desperation.

'You also said that you wouldn't marry…"someone like me" I believe was the term you used.'

She winced, and then up came her chin. 'So I changed my mind? It would be better if you could just forget some of the stuff I said that morning.'

'I have a photographic memory. To recap—marriage is your condition?'

'Gosh, did it sound like I was pointing a loaded shotgun at you?'

Not a flicker of expression revealed Cristiano's opinion on that score. 'It's my first proposal. I have no basis for comparison.'

Mortification was welling up through her like a fountain. 'You are obviously trying to avoid saying no. That's okay—don't worry about it. I'm really not bothered,' she framed as jaggedly as broken glass.

Cristiano cleared his throat.

It belatedly dawned on Lydia that the chauffeur had opened the door for her to alight. She scrambled out and headed at a speedy rate of knots into the *palazzo*. She was so embarrassed she wanted to curl up and die. She had asked him to marry her! How could she have done that? All right, so she had regretted turning him down outright. She'd known that even the direst torture would not persuade him to mention the idea again. But she should've been more subtle. Tears of hurt and anger were stinging her eyes.

Abruptly she spun back to him in the hall. 'It's because you think I'm a thief, isn't it? Well, maybe that's not as cut and dried as you believe. I mean…maybe I *didn't* take the money! Has that idea ever occurred to you? Did you ever wonder what I did with two hundred and fifty grand when I was renting a house that would fit under your stairs?'

'On several occasions,' Cristiano admitted. 'You have

no decent jewellery, no expensive possessions, and from what I have so far seen no extravagant habits. But you could have been in serious debt.'

Lydia had fallen silent. She worried at the soft under-side of her full lower lip. She hated him thinking that she was dishonest. At the outset of their relationship she had been too desperate for help to worry, and too bitter to care about his opinion of her. But now Cristi-ano's view of her mattered a great deal, and she really did want to tell him the truth. After all, now the missing funds had been replaced, she reasoned anxiously, did she need to continue the pretence that she had stolen the charity money?

Just as quickly as she thought that, she realised that she still had good reason for keeping quiet on that score. Cristiano could be very black and white in his outlook, un-forgiving and intolerant of shades of grey. Suppose she admitted the truth and he decided to report her mother to the police? Was that still possible? She had no idea. But she did suspect that Cristiano would react badly to the news. Trusting him with too much information might com-promise everything she had so far done to protect Virginia. Right now, Cristiano was not only keen to help her find her mother, but he also had the resources to do so. If she admitted that Virginia was the guilty party who had helped herself to charitable funds, would he still be so willing? It was certain to affect his attitude. At the very least he would be furious that she had let him credit a lie.

Cristiano pressed a firm hand to her slender spine and urged her into the grand drawing room. He leant back against the door, his shrewd gaze intent on her troubled face. 'You're wondering whether or not to tell me some-thing, *bella mia*. Let me make that decision for you. Now that I know that there's a secret, there will be no peace on this earth for you until you tell all.'

'There's no secret…' Suddenly the very last thing Lydia wanted to do was open a controversial subject that would annoy him.

'You can tell me anything.'

'There's nothing to tell.'

'It's a very bad idea to lie to me,' Cristiano warned her with chilling softness, dark eyes shorn of gold enticement. 'You're not a good liar either.'

Her colour fluctuated, a tight knot of alarm forming in her tummy. The atmosphere had dropped several degrees in the blink of an eye. 'It's not something that would hurt you.'

'Perhaps I'm not prepared to let you make that judgement call.'

'Please…it's not important,' she protested.

'If I'm going to marry you, I need to know I can trust you. So you think about that angle, and work out whether or not you have something you want to share with me,' Cristiano advised with devastating cool as he walked over to the tall window and swung back round to face her.

'That's blackmail!' Lydia condemned in consternation.

Cristiano shrugged with magnificent disregard of the effect that it would have on restoring peaceful relations. 'It is me telling you like it is.'

'I don't want to marry you anyway!' she launched back at him in angry frustration.

Cristiano released a weary groan. '*Dio mio,* please don't start that refrain again.'

'Why? Do you find it so hard to believe that I wouldn't want to marry you?'

Brilliant golden eyes struck literal sparks off her challenging blue gaze. 'I have my reasons.'

'Explain those reasons.'

'I don't want to.'

'I don't like secrets either.'

'Let's wind this down,' Cristiano breathed with sudden impatience. 'This is not a conversation we need to have—'

'Yes, it is. I want to know why you are so certain that I want to marry you!'

Cristiano shifted lean brown hands in a silencing gesture. 'This is getting very childish.'

If anything, that comment only made Lydia even angrier. 'You shouldn't say things that you can't justify.'

Cristiano shot her a glittering glance, strode over to the desk, extracted something from a drawer and set it out. 'You shouldn't challenge me…'

Lydia stared at the familiar photo, which she had last seen when she was packing up her possessions in Wales. Immediately she realised that she must have overlooked it and left it lying on the windowsill. Confronted with it in Italy, however, she could not credit her eyesight and was literally struck dumb. Where had he got it from?

Cristiano watched every scrap of colour ebb from beneath her translucent skin and cursed his competitive instincts and his temper. He wondered why his cool logic always let him down around her. As he approached her she sidestepped him in an abrupt movement, snatched up the old photo frame and clasped it in front of her.

'I shouldn't have shown you,' he said flatly.

'How did you get hold of this? I think you owe me an explanation for that at least.'

He told her about Gwenna's visit to his office.

She swallowed hard, imagining how shocked her cousin would have been by that contract. Gwenna certainly wouldn't have intended to embarrass her. But that Cristiano should have seen that photograph stripped Lydia of all pride. Her biggest secret, and Cristiano now knew that he had been her idol when she was a brainless little teenager, with nothing better to do than mope over a guy she'd never met. Her sense of humiliation knew no bounds. For goodness' sake, had her cousin also let drop that Lydia had referred to Cristiano as the love of her life?

Feeling literally sick with mortification, she yanked open the door.

'Lydia…' Cristiano breathed. 'Where are you going?'

'I need fresh air!' She raced down the hall, pausing only to scoop up the keys of the sports car he had said she was free to use.

'I don't want you driving in the mood you're in!'

Nothing could have made Lydia more determined to get into a car.

The sleek little Lamborghini gunned down the long drive at a satisfying pace—fast enough to give him pause for thought—but she slowed right down the minute she rounded a corner and was no longer within sight. That wretched juvenile picture of him! Why had she ever kept it? Her teeth gritted. She headed up the steep twisting road to the little fortified hill town at the top.

Parking the car beside a medieval church, she walked down a flight of worn steps to the sunny *piazza*. She ordered a soft drink at the wine bar where she had sat with Cristiano one evening a week earlier. Everyone who'd walked by had known him. The local priest had joined them for a glass of wine. There had been a constant procession of people wandering up to exchange news with Cristiano. She had noticed that here in the town he had known since childhood he was very relaxed.

She loved him, she conceded ruefully. So what if he

suspected that? Was her pride more important to her than her happiness? And hadn't he been right to say that if they were going to marry they should have no secrets from each other? Now that her angry mortification had had a chance to cool, she was willing to admit that she liked that idea. That was a good solid principle on which to base a relationship—so why was she refusing to trust him with the truth about the Happy Holidays money?

Cristiano brought his Ferrari to a far from cool halt beside the Lamborghini and leapt out. He could not understand why he had shown her that photo. It had been a bloody insensitive thing to do! But why had she taken off like that? Where was she? He glanced inside the church. He strode over to the low wall which warned the unwary of the sheer terrifying drop into the valley far below. If anything had happened to her, he would never forgive himself.

A wolf-whistle sounded in the hot still air and he swung round to see where it had come from. He saw her from the top of the steps. She was an exquisitely feminine vision in a mint skirt and a sleeveless top. His heartbeat steadied again. The kid who had whistled waved at him from the *piazza* and ran off laughing.

When she saw Cristiano crossing the *piazza*, her mouth ran dry. He was so very Italian, in his elegant, beautifully cut white shirt and cream chinos, and looked absolutely gorgeous with sunshine gilding his ebony hair and superb bone structure.

'May I sit down?'

'Well, you've chased off the competition…that little boy will go far.'

'He knew you were already taken, *gioia mia*.'

Her sapphire-blue eyes glimmered. 'Is that a fact?'

'I'm sorry I upset you,' he breathed tautly. 'But I

thought it was really sweet that you had a photo of me at that age. I was honoured, and very touched.'

Her cheeks warmed, for his words still stung. He had probably guessed that she loved him. Why else would he be honoured and touched? A guy notorious for his lack of heart? *Sweet*? He felt sorry for her, didn't he? Here she was, she had fallen like a ton of bricks for him before she even met him, and after all this time he was still the only man she had ever cared about! She decided that a change of subject would be her wisest move.

'I've got something to tell you,' she announced once the barman had poured their wine and returned to reading his newspaper in the sunshine. 'It wasn't me who took the charity money. It was my mum…'

Cristiano studied her with frowning force, not a muscle moving in his bold bronzed features. For a split second he closed his eyes, and then he released his breath in a slow ragged exhalation.

'My stepfather, Dennis, left her with a lot of debt, and she borrowed from the charity account. Of course she didn't think through the reality—that once she'd settled bills with the money she had no way of replacing it.'

His bronzed complexion had developed a pale cast. 'But why didn't you tell me this weeks ago?'

'I would've told you eventually, but at the start I couldn't imagine us being together even this long,' she confessed. 'I didn't really care what you thought of me either. I was worried sick about Mum. I only accepted your financial help when I realised that the police intended to track her down and question her.'

Cristiano looked grave. 'You could have told me the truth.'

'I didn't actually think you would be that interested in whether or not I was guilty.'

His lean powerful face tightened at that admission.

'And I didn't trust you,' Lydia admitted ruefully. 'How did I know how you would react? You might have gone and told all to the police just on principle. I kept it secret to protect my mother. And even now I feel bad about telling you. I don't want you to think badly of her.'

'I can't imagine why I would do that,' Cristiano murmured stonily, pushing his empty glass away. 'Why would I think badly of a woman who stole a quarter of a million from underprivileged children and left her daughter to face the music?'

Lydia directed a look of reproach at him and watched him pay for the wine. They mounted the steps from the *piazza* together. 'I've never been anything but bad luck for my mother, and I was more than willing to do whatever it took to help her when she needed me,' she admitted tautly. 'Please try to understand that it was my choice.'

'Including making the ultimate sacrifice in my bed?' Cristiano vented an unamused laugh and raked a rough hand through his cropped black hair, his lean, vibrantly handsome face bleak. 'When I said I owed you, a few weeks ago, I had no idea how much.'

'You don't owe me anything. I chose to mislead you. And if you find out where my mother is now, I'll be forever grateful.'

'That's the least of what I can do. Get in the Ferrari. Arnaldo can bring the Lamborghini back.'

Lydia climbed into the passenger seat of his car. 'Does it ever occur to you that, as sacrifices go, I'm a reasonably happy one?'

Brooding dark golden eyes met hers levelly. 'I wanted you at any price, *bella mia*. Honour and decency didn't come into it until it was too late to change anything. I'll always regret that.' He drove the powerful car down the hill at a speed that she would not have dared on a straight road, never mind a twisting one. 'But I promise that no matter what it takes I'll find your mother for you.'

Her wide warm smile began to blossom. 'And you won't report her to the police or anything?'

'I doubt that they'd be interested when there's no charge left to answer.'

Back at the *palazzo*, Lydia hovered several inches from him, helpfully within reach. She wanted him to haul her into his arms and drag her off to bed, or make mad passionate love to her on the spot. He didn't usually require encouragement. She felt slightly foolish when he said that he had some phone calls to make.

She dined alone that evening, and went to bed early, on the principle that he deserved to have to come looking for her.

She rose early the next morning, distinctly troubled by Cristiano's failure to put in an appearance. She went for a stroll in the dappled shade of the trees. At that hour the gardens were cool and silent. She was relieved when she emerged from a tranquil green arbour of vines and saw Cristiano striding towards her.

He came to a halt several feet away. 'I have an address for your mother!'

Lydia was astonished. 'My word—how did you manage to find that out so soon?'

Cristiano told her about the report he had ordered several weeks earlier. She nodded, not particularly concerned, because she was much more interested in learning Virginia's whereabouts. The report had contained a lead that he had had followed up. 'France?' she repeated. 'Okay—so…'

'The jet's on standby. We'll leave at noon, *cara mia.*'

A huge smile curved her soft full mouth. 'How am I ever going to thank you for this?'

It seemed to her that his lean dark features shadowed, but when he closed his hands over hers and tugged her into his arms she believed she must have been mistaken. He gazed down at her, stunning dark golden eyes very serious. 'You can say thank you by marrying me, *carissima*.'

'Yes…oh, yes,' she said immediately, and she thought he might laugh at the speed of her response but he didn't.

'I want to do it all by the book. We'll throw a massive engagement party so that I can show you off to all my friends.'

Misgivings stirred, in spite of her attempt to stay totally positive. Was he only marrying her because he felt he owed it to her?

Signing her up to a contract had definitely given him the chance to get in touch with his conscience, she reflected worriedly. Here she was, like Faithful Penelope in the legend, not quite growing old waiting for him, but certainly in the dogged and devoted category. But why shouldn't he like that? And when he had decided he'd like to be a father, why not choose her? After all, as he had so freely admitted, he didn't do love.

He eased her into the shelter of his lean powerful body and showed her what he *did* do. It wasn't love, she acknowledged, but even before he savoured her ripe mouth she literally couldn't breathe for excitement.

'Don't stop,' she mumbled between frantic kisses, backing up against the trunk of a tree, every inch of her exuding weak, wanton invitation.

'We must,' Cristiano sighed. 'I've invited a friend in the jewellery trade to call with a selection of rings.'

The speed with which everything was happening continued to surprise Lydia. Cristiano was usually a cautious guy. Now he was suggesting that the engagement party be staged within a fortnight and the wedding date be set immediately. In a magnificent reception room in the *palazzo*, she agonised with immense enjoyment over a gorgeous choice of rings, before finally choosing a ravishing diamond cluster that she adored.

Lydia was so excited at the prospect of seeing her mother again and introducing Cristiano to her that she couldn't settle during the flight. She flicked through magazines and picked at her lunch.

Cristiano was very quiet, and when she finally noticed that it bothered her.

'Is there something the matter?' Lydia asked in the limo that picked them up at the airport.

'I think you may be in for a few surprises when you see your mother.'

She tensed. 'What sort of surprises?'

'She would appear to be living with your stepfather—Dennis.'

'Oh, my word—have they got back together again? That's wonderful…she'll be over the moon!' Lydia declared with satisfaction.

Cristiano reached for her hand. 'I can't let you walk into this unprepared—'

'Unprepared for what?'

'I believe that you've been the victim of some very cruel scams. I've checked out certain facts. That nightclub in which you invested did not go bust to the tune of anything like the amount of money you lost. I think your stepfather used the club venture to strip you of your savings.'

Lydia studied him in horror. 'Are you serious? You honestly believe Dennis is a crook?'

'He's a conman with a criminal record for petty theft.'

'But he's an accountant—'

'He has no professional qualifications. I'm afraid I also suspect that Dennis did not work alone. I know you don't want to hear this,' Cristiano imparted grimly. 'But all the evidence that I've seen indicates that your mother was fully involved at every level—'

'Stop it—you're right, I don't want to hear it!' Lydia told him, more in dismay than anger. 'You're a terribly cynical person, Cristiano. I'm willing to believe that Dennis is dishonest, but not my mother too.'

The limo had come to a halt while a member of Cristiano's security team spoke into the intercom beside a tall wooden gate. Beyond it she could see the roofline of a substantial villa.

'But this can't be where they're living,' she reasoned when the gate opened and the car moved forward again. 'The police had got hold of some mad rumour about a big house in France as well. I think we're on a wild-goose chase.'

'It wasn't a rumour. Dennis and Virginia had to disappear to enjoy their ill-gotten gains,' Cristiano advanced harshly. 'They go by the names of Janette and Brian Carson here. Your stepfather has set up as a property developer.'

'This can't possibly be my mother's home. It's a case of mistaken identity…it's got to be! If Virginia had this kind of money, why would she have taken the Happy Holidays funds? How could she have been in debt? Why would she have begged me to tell the police that *I* took the missing cash?'

'Greed. A last little sting before they embarked on their new life as well-heeled ex-pats. You'd never have heard from them again.'

'You are wrong…' Lydia almost fell out of the car in her haste to vacate it.

A middle-aged maid answered the door. Behind her, Lydia saw her mother, clad in a sunhat and a stylish shift dress.

'Lydia?' Virginia studied her daughter in horror. 'I thought it was a furniture delivery! How did you get in? How did you find us?'

and barmaid winked. A chilling inevitability had descended
him, but now to access the information he sought...

Lydia wondered whether she'd recount his emotions, yet
she could not recall a word she was about to speak. She laced
his hand within her own...in a strengthening manner,
almost as if she hoped...some encouragement to answer it
seek that to proceed.

CHAPTER TEN

LYDIA was trembling. She was afraid to look at her mother,
and found it easier at that moment to appraise her surroundings instead. What she saw shattered her hope that
there might be an acceptable explanation. This was definitely Virginia's home. The paintings, sculptures and luxurious furniture were all recognisably in her parent's
theatrical decorative taste.

'Did Dennis ever walk out on you? Or was that just part
of the sob story you fed me?' Lydia enquired tightly.

'We've just reconciled,' Virginia said shrilly.

Unimpressed by that claim, Lydia walked past the older
woman into a spacious reception room. Her stepfather,
wearing shorts that did not flatter his rotund dimensions,
was watching football there, on a giant plasma screen.
When he saw his stepdaughter his jaw dropped.

'Where did you get the money for all this?' Lydia asked
her mother painfully.

Cristiano appeared in the doorway.

'Who on earth have you brought with you?' Virginia lit
a cigarette with a bold flourish.

'Never mind who he is. You told me you were in debt

and broke, but that was obviously untrue,' Lydia continued tightly. 'For how long have you owned this villa?'

'We're only minding this house,' the older woman told her.

'The villa is in your mother's name. She bought it with cash a couple of years ago,' Cristiano contradicted drily. 'You were a very generous daughter, but they wanted everything you had. They siphoned off thousands from your bank accounts.'

'That's a dirty lie!' Her stepfather's heavy face was brick-red.

Cristiano dealt him a look of derision. 'You left a paper trail of evidence any good accountant could follow. Moderate your tone and your attitude. Lydia has enough documentary proof to put both of you in prison for fraud for a good few years.'

'But she won't do it,' Virginia declared, with a complacent smile of challenge. 'I'm her mother, and what was hers is mine. Didn't you often tell me that, Lydia?'

Lydia found that she was both hurt and shamed by her mother's behaviour. Clearly the older couple had been stealing from her for a very long time, but Virginia's blue eyes, which were so eerily like her own, remained hard and defiant. There was no apology, no regret there.

'Didn't you care that I might go to prison for your crime?' Lydia could not help whispering.

The blonde woman made no answer.

Lydia could feel tears welling up, and she fought them with all her might. In that silence lay her answer. Gwenna had once called her the family cash cow, and now she saw the truth of that wounding label. She had been valued only for the money she could bring home. Recalling how much

Virginia and Dennis had resented her decision to retire from modelling, she almost shuddered. When the cash cow had run dry they had had to devise new ways of stripping her of her savings.

With as much dignity as she could muster, Lydia walked straight-backed out of the villa and climbed into the limo. It moved off, and she stared out of the window with blank eyes. Fierce emotion was warring within her. Then, without a word, she scrambled along the seat and flung herself into Cristiano's arms. He said nothing, which was fortunate, for she believed that words of sympathy would make her break down completely. Her eyes burned but she didn't cry.

'She never loved me…and deep down inside I always knew it too,' she muttered chokily. 'But I used to try so hard to please her.'

'I won't let her hurt you ever again, *gioia mia*.'

He held her close and she shut her eyes tight, loving him with so much force and passion she quivered. Desperate to offer something back, she said, 'I'll try getting on your yacht again…okay?'

Above her head, Cristiano drew in a slow deep breath. He smoothed her tumbled hair in a soothing gesture. 'Maybe some time. It's really not important.'

The helicopter flew over the vast roof that distinguished Cristiano's country home in England. Welbrooke Park was a very beautiful country house, and as the helicopter landed Lydia was recalling her last fateful visit, which had concluded with her early-morning departure in Mort Stevens's ridiculously small sports car. She smiled ruefully

at that tragi-comic memory. The agony of pain and disil-
lusionment she had suffered that weekend was far behind
her now. In a couple of hours she would be greeting the
guests invited to their engagement celebrations.

Cristiano, who had been in London on business for two
days, strode out of the drawing room to greet her. 'Come
and meet some of my friends,' he imparted, and then, half
under his breath, 'Sorry, I had hoped to have you to myself
for a while, but it's not to be.'

Preceding him into the room, she stiffened when she
saw Philip Hazlett, but relaxed when she was introduced
to his languid fiancée, Jodie.

'Quite the miracle-worker, aren't you?' Philip remarked
under cover of the general conversation. 'You went from
rank outsider to winner and took us all by surprise.'

'I'm not sure I understand.'

The thickset banker vented a suggestive laugh. 'Who
wouldn't be impressed? A bimbo with a beautiful body has
caught one of the world's richest men. I can only assume
that you're a real goer in the bedroom!'

Lydia reddened, realising in dismay that her unease in
Philip's radius eighteen months earlier had been well
founded. Some sixth sense had warned her that he was a
creep even before she'd heard him discussing that
infamous bet. 'Don't speak to me like that.'

'If I'd come along before Cristiano, you'd have been
singing a very different tune,' Philip asserted with unmistakable meaning.

'No…never in this lifetime.' Lydia could not hide her
look of revulsion, and she saw angry resentment harden
his florid face before she turned gratefully away.

So that, she thought with an inner shudder, was what she had sensed in Philip Hazlett. He had been attracted to her, and seeing her with Cristiano would've annoyed him—for Philip cherished a high opinion of himself. He was charm personified with women he accepted as his equals, but an ignorant swine with those he considered to be socially beneath him. What a shame that he should be such a close friend of Cristiano's, she reflected uncomfortably. She wasn't planning to tell tales. But Philip would have to get over his need to put her down.

Cristiano strode into the bedroom when she was fresh out of the shower. His dark golden eyes glittered and her tummy flipped, because she knew what that smouldering look meant.

'You smell wonderful,' he breathed, pulling her back against him with single-minded purpose.

'Soap.'

Laughing huskily, he brushed her glorious hair out of his path and pressed his sensual mouth to her neck. A little gasp broke from her lips and she trembled. After forty-eight hours without him, sudden contact made her feel shamelessly wanton. 'My hair and my make-up still have to be done,' she muttered, more than willing to be over-ruled.

'I know…and I won't make you late tonight, *cara mia*.' Cristiano set her back from him with a distinct air of self-denial. 'Maybe I'll drag you into a dark corner around midnight. I don't think I can restrain myself much longer than that. I missed you so much.'

Later, Gwenna came to keep Lydia company.

'So, tell me, what do you think of Cristiano?' Lydia asked almost shyly.

Gwenna pulled a comical face. 'He's a good sport. When I cornered him in his office, he kept his cool.'

'You like him?'

'What woman *wouldn't* like him? He spent fifteen minutes talking to me downstairs. I felt really important. He's a total babe!'

'Gwenna!' Lydia laughed.

'With that amount of charisma, he's definitely a catch.'

'His friend Philip would certainly agree with that. Unfortunately he sees me as a bimbo, who used sex to trap his mate into marriage,' Lydia confided with a grimace.

'Surely the dreadful man didn't dare to say that to your face?'

Lydia told her story, her wounded feelings soothed by Gwenna's annoyance on her behalf. Predictably, Gwenna thought she should tell Cristiano, but Lydia grimaced at the idea. She knew she was probably being silly, but she was scared that if she repeated Philip's comments Cristiano might start wondering whether there were any grains of truth in his friend's derisive opinion of his approaching nuptials. When men talked with other men about such things they could really be quite obnoxious, she thought worriedly, her memory dwelling on that ghastly betting business. Even Cristiano had not been proof against the masculine need to seem ultra-cool and callous. Did some sort of pack instinct come out in guys when they got together?

An hour later Lydia, stunning in a magnificent pale

green ball gown that bared her shoulders, descended the wonderful Georgian staircase. Diamonds sparkled like white fire at her ears, throat and wrist. The society photographer waiting to record her appearance took several shots and Cristiano, the very epitome of sleek male fashion, in a cutting-edge designer suit and open-necked black shirt, joined her for another few.

Philip Hazlett was in the crowd of guests watching the photo session, and she glimpsed his sour expression before hurriedly looking away, determined not to let anything spoil her engagement party.

Cristiano whirled her round the ballroom. 'You're on edge, and it's not like you.'

Lydia rested her brow against his shoulder. She was getting really annoyed with herself. It was a wonderful party, and their guests were having a terrific time. Only Philip had been rude. Why was she letting that bother her so much? Was she getting precious? Did she expect everyone to like and approve of her?

But she knew what was the matter with her, didn't she?

Being reminded that all she had to offer Cristiano was her body had been painful. He wasn't in love with her, and that made her feel insecure and vulnerable. Love was like a glue that could keep people together through rain and shine. Cristiano, however, was perfectly happy to settle for amazing sex. He had discovered that he wanted a child, and she had been in the right place at the right time when he decided that he would like to try settling down. That was why she had a dazzling diamond on her engagement finger. But with such a foundation wasn't he likely to get bored with her? And, when he did, what would they use for glue? *Her* love?

Around midnight, she noticed that Gwenna was still dancing with the same man and she smiled. Feeling warm, and wondering where Cristiano was, she walked through the house to the suite of offices he used. She was already deciding what she was going to say if she found him there working when he shouldn't be. The rooms, however, were in darkness. Beyond the windows the gardens had been transformed with glimmering fibre-optic lights. She was thinking how beautiful it looked, and grinning at the sight of the young man being chased by not one but two giggling girls across the lawn, when she heard a noise behind her.

'I thought I'd never get you on your own.'

Lydia spun round, her oval face taut.

Philip Hazlett was leering at her from the doorway. 'What will Cristiano think if he finds you've been down here with me? We've been friends all our lives. He trusts me like a brother. Who do you think he'll believe if I say you were flirting like mad and gagging for it?'

Cold apprehension clutched at Lydia. She could feel his menace. She could feel him savouring her fear. If she screamed it was unlikely anyone would hear her above the music emanating from the party. Philip was blocking the only exit, and he was built like a concrete cube of muscle.

'I'm meeting Cristiano here.'

Philip advanced. 'Don't waste your breath. He's in the main hall, talking business over a brandy.'

Lydia took a sidewise step, staying out of reach, her heart thumping so hard inside her chest that she felt sick. 'Stay away from me—'

'You'll be too scared to tell him I've had you. You have too much to lose,' he asserted smugly. 'It'll be our little secret for evermore…'

Lydia jerked as she saw movement behind Philip. Someone flipped him round and hit him so fast and hard that he crashed down like a felled tree. Trembling, she just stood there gaping as Philip leapt back up—only to be flattened a second time with an even harder punch.

'You filthy bastard!' Cristiano growled, only backing off to extend a strong supportive arm round Lydia, whose state of shock was patent. 'If you had laid one finger on her I'd have killed you for it! But you frightened her, and that's bad enough. I'm calling the police—'

'No—no police,' Lydia mumbled unevenly. 'He didn't touch me. Don't him let him spoil the party. Just get him out of here!'

Arnaldo gave her an approving nod and anchored a hand like a giant meat hook in Philip's jacket, to remove him from the scene.

Lydia was shaking like a leaf. 'How did you know I was here?'

'Arnaldo was keeping an eye on you and on Philip all evening. I suspected Philip had said something to you when you arrived. You went all quiet, and I noticed the freaky way he was watching you. It wasn't the first time I'd noticed his interest in you.' His strong jawline squared. 'He always wanted you, *bella mia*.'

'You *knew* that?'

Cristiano gave her a rueful look as he shepherded her out into the corridor. 'Look in the mirror. *All* my friends wanted you. I couldn't make it a hanging offence. I didn't think anything of it eighteen months ago. But this time around, with Philip engaged to Jodie, I found it offensive and rather disturbing.'

'I thought he was your best friend.'

'Did he tell you that? I've tolerated him because I do a lot of business with his father, who is everything the son is not. I have nothing in common with Philip now. What friendship we had left withered over that crass bet. Tonight...' Cristiano paused, his dark golden gaze gleaming over her pallor and hardening to cold steel. 'Tonight I could have killed him.'

'I was really scared—'

'Blame me for that. I had no idea that he might have an assault in mind,' Cristiano breathed with fierce regret. 'I thought he might be pestering you and making a nuisance of himself. I intended to put a stop to it. But you were never in any danger. Arnaldo would have intervened had I not arrived.'

'I suppose we should go back to our guests.'

But Cristiano directed her up a flight of service stairs. 'They don't need us present to party. You've had an unpleasant experience and you need time to recover from that. If that bastard had managed to touch you—'

'But he *didn't*...' Stretching up on tiptoe on the landing, Lydia rested a placating finger against his parted lips. 'I'm unhurt and I'm okay—'

'No thanks to me. I can't even keep you safe from harm under my own roof,' Cristiano growled in a driven voice. 'I'll also have to tell Jodie about what happened. She's an old friend, and it would be wrong to keep it from her.'

'If she loves him, she may not want to know.'

'Thankfully, that's not our business.'

On the threshold of their bedroom, Cristiano scooped Lydia up into his arms and carried her over to the bed, where he laid her down with gentle hands. He studied her with brooding intensity, as if he still wasn't quite sure that she really was all right.

'Will you stop blaming yourself?' she sighed. 'I'm fine—right as rain—fighting fit!'

'Of course I'm blaming myself!' Cristiano fielded without hesitation. 'I didn't appreciate what a nutter Philip was. I seem to screw up everything with you!'

'No, you don't.'

Cristiano looked unconvinced. He moved away several feet, turned in a restless arc like a lion confined in too small a space. 'There are some things I need to tell you…'

Lydia sat up in readiness. Cristiano stared at her, then looked away again, almost imperceptible colour scoring his taut cheekbones.

'Yes…?' Lydia prompted.

'I haven't been straight with you or with myself. I fell in love with you almost two years ago. I saw you on that catwalk and then I heard your voice, saw the way you put your head to one side when you speak. There was just something so unbelievably appealing about you,' he confided, seemingly unaware that she was now studying him with a dropped jaw. 'But I didn't realise that what you made me feel was love, because I hated the trapped feeling it gave me.'

'The…trapped feeling?' Lydia echoed, thrust back down to earth again with a nasty bump. Had he really said what she thought he had? Or had her imagination taken a gigantic leap all on its own?

'I don't think I was ready for anything serious. You got inside my head and spooked me. *Dio mio,* I'd be in a meeting and then *bang*—out of nowhere I'd find that I was thinking about you!' he recalled with a shudder that spoke volumes. 'All my focus would be gone. It was a nightmare. So when I wanted to see you I would make myself wait longer. That way I stayed in control of events.'

'So I was right to blame you for not making more effort to see me.'

'I showed how interested I was in other ways,' Cristiano countered. 'I bought you roses. I even sent you a card on Valentine's Day.'

'It was a black and white picture of New York with your name in it and no message—'

Cristiano wasn't listening. 'I also phoned you all the time. That was serious new territory for me.'

'I'm surprised that fact didn't wake you up in the night in a cold sweat!'

'All that woke me up was the need for a cold shower, because you weren't there in my bed with me, *bella mia*.'

Lydia went pink. 'When I overheard Philip talking about that horrible bet, it wrecked everything.'

'That was all my fault.' His lean, darkly handsome face was bleak with recollection. 'I'm sorry you were hurt, but if it's any consolation it was a body-blow when you took off with Mort Stevens. I was gutted. Life lost all its flavour, and I didn't work out why until very recently. But I did have a recurring fantasy in which you came to me on your knees, begging to be taken back, *cara mia*.'

Lydia was perched on the side of the bed, her entire attention lodged on him. 'Is that why you turned fantasy into fact when you heard I was in trouble?'

'And the next time I got you in my sights I made sure there was no way you could leave me a second time.'

'The contract?' Now that its purpose had been fully explained, Lydia felt almost fond of that part of their history.

'I wanted you tied hand and foot to me, so that you couldn't walk away again.'

'Obviously somewhere along the line you got acclimatised to that trapped feeling,' Lydia remarked.

'Losing you to Stevens was a painful cure. Although I got you back into my life, I couldn't forget that you'd walked out on me…'

'The first time you proposed—?'

Cristiano vented a rueful laugh. 'It was a disaster. I was all over the place. I hadn't thought anything through. I felt so guilty, and I wanted to keep you with me. But I thought you hated me and that made me arrogant.'

Her nose wrinkled. 'I thought I hated you too.'

'When Gwenna showed me that photo you'd kept of me, it was like a shot of adrenalin. I was so low,' he confessed. 'I wasn't getting anywhere with you. But it seemed to me that if you'd felt that way about me once, there was still hope. When you got the wrong idea about that Russian model, I was delighted.'

Her eyes were radiant, for she was looking back and recognising how hard he had worked to win her trust and love. Sliding off the bed, she walked over to him and slid her hands up to his shoulders. 'When did you start *really* wanting to marry me?'

'Probably the moment you said no.' His stunning gold eyes rested intently on her lovely face. 'I need to know you're mine. I won't feel safe until you've signed our marriage certificate in triplicate in two weeks' time.'

'What if I asked you to sign a contract?' she teased.

His handsome dark head lowered, for he was mesmerised by the tantalising smile on her soft pink mouth. 'It would depend on the terms.'

'You have to love me as much as I love you.'

'*Do* you love me?' Cristiano searched her eyes with wondering appreciation. 'I thought I still had to work on that angle.'

'Actually, you didn't have to work half as hard as you deserved. That teenage crush of mine worked in your favour.' Lydia traced a high masculine cheekbone with loving appreciation, her fingers gentle. 'I told myself I hated you to protect myself from getting hurt again, and then I had to accept that I still loved you.'

'I'll never give you cause to regret it,' Cristiano swore, with a raw sincerity that touched her to the heart.

He claimed her mouth in a long, drugging kiss. The instant physical contact was renewed, their overwhelming need to express their love in passion drove every other consideration from their minds.

The host and hostess did not reappear downstairs until dawn was high in the sky.

Eighteen months later, Lydia gave her daughter, Bella, a last tender kiss and tucked her in for the night. Bella was two months old and her dark blue eyes were drowsy. Within minutes the gentle rocking of the cradle sent her to sleep. She was a very pretty baby, with black hair that lay like a silk cap on her pale skin, and a tiny serene face.

Standing with a glass of wine on the terrace an hour later, Lydia savoured the peace and the view across the Tuscan valley that now, more than any other place, felt like home to her.

Two weeks after their engagement party she and Cristiano

had exchanged rings and vows in the little candlelit church on the hill. It had been very much a private affair, hushed up to keep the paparazzi at bay and attended by only a chosen few. Gwenna had been her only attendant. Jodie, who had ditched Philip Hazlett, had attended with her latest boy-friend. Lydia had worn fluid white silk georgette, and the An-dreotti diamond tiara had come out of the bank vault for the occasion. A single photo of the bride and groom on the church steps had been released to the press. The happy couple had spent their honeymoon on a private island in Greece, enjoying the feeling that they were getting back to nature while actually living in the lap of luxury.

The period since then had been one of great happiness for Lydia. In six weeks Gwenna was getting married to the businessman she had met at the engagement party. Cristiano had endowed the Happy Holidays charity with a house in Cornwall, and the funds to keep it running for the children. Lydia had presided over the official opening and had done sufficient fundraising to have long since forgotten her former embarrassment around the staff.

Of course there had been one or two more trying moments in their lives as well. In that category Lydia included Virginia's frantic appeal for the name of a good lawyer after she and Dennis were arrested by the French police and held in custody for dubious property deals. Everything the couple possessed had since been seized, and a prison sentence for them both looked unavoidable. Cristiano had made one or two pithy comments about justice being done.

There had also been the time that Lydia had snatched Cristiano's mobile phone from him and chucked it in the sea. She had got away with that because it had been the same day that he'd managed to persuade her to paddle in the surf. Since then she had reached the stage where she could fool about in the shallow end of a pool without suffering a panic attack, and she had been on *Lestara* twice for brief cruises. Bit by bit she was overcoming her fear, but she couldn't have come so far without Cristiano's support and patience.

A warm smile curved Lydia's lips when she heard the distant chop-chop of the helicopter approaching. It was Cristiano, flying back from a meeting in London. She heard his steps ringing across the tiled hall inside the house and her heartbeat picked up pace the way it always did when he was near.

When he appeared on the terrace, she flung herself into his arms without hesitation. Releasing a hungry groan, he held her to him and kissed her breathless.

'It's so uncool when we do this. Our friends would be shocked. No wonder we don't entertain much.' Closing a lean hand over hers, Cristiano took a long, appreciative look at her. 'How's Bella?'

'Fast asleep.'

'I guarantee she won't be at three in the morning,' her father forecast. 'Knowing that, I came home with all possible haste. We can have an early night and still be fresh for our darling daughter when she wakes up in the middle of the night.'

'But it's only eight o'clock.'

A provocative smile slashed his lean dark features. 'I know.'

She burst out laughing.

'London was a desert without you,' Cristiano confided.

'Every time I have to leave you I find out all over again how much I love you, *gioia mia*.'

Happiness lighting her face, Lydia glowed beneath the tender look in his stunning eyes. As she settled back into his arms she had not a care in the world—for she had found her place…

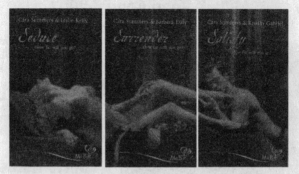

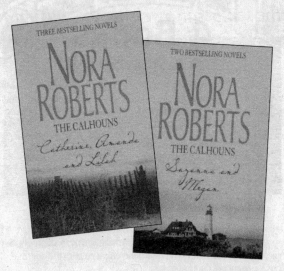

4 Books
and a surprise gift!

We would like to take this opportunity to thank you for reading this Mills & Boon® book by offering you the chance to take FOUR more specially selected titles from the Modern Romance™ series absolutely FREE! We're also making this offer to introduce you to the benefits of the Mills & Boon® Reader Service™—

- ★ **FREE home delivery**
- ★ **FREE gifts and competitions**
- ★ **FREE monthly Newsletter**
- ★ **Exclusive Reader Service offers**
- ★ **Books available before they're in the shops**

Accepting these FREE books and gift places you under no obligation to buy, you may cancel at any time, even after receiving your free shipment. Simply complete your details below and return the entire page to the address below. You don't even need a stamp!

YES! Please send me 4 free Modern Romance books and a surprise gift. I understand that unless you hear from me, I will receive 6 superb new titles every month for just £2.80 each, postage and packing free. I am under no obligation to purchase any books and may cancel my subscription at any time. The free books and gift will be mine to keep in any case.

P6ZEF

Ms/Mrs/Miss/Mr ....Initials............................

Surname .... **BLOCK CAPITALS PLEASE**

Address ....

....

....Postcode ....

Send this whole page to:
UK: FREEPOST CN81, Croydon, CR9 3WZ